We Speak CHICAGOESE

stories and poems by Chicago writers

Edited by Bill Donlon and Dennis Foley

A SIDE STREET PRESS BOOK
Published by
Side Street Press Inc.
3400 West 111th Street, #412
Chicago, IL 60655

SIDESTREETPRESSInc.
www.sidestreetpressinc.com

ISBN: 978-0-692-65885-7

Printed in the United States of America

First Edition: June, 2016

Cover art and photographs by Patrick Foley

ACKNOWLEDGEMENT

Thanks to Maggie Carson for reviewing the submitted material. Your thoughts, suggestions, edits, corrections and time are truly appreciated.

Table of Contents

Introduction

Is CHICAGOESE an actual language? In our opinion, the answer is a resounding and definitive, YES! In the pages that follow, Chicago authors and poets will fill your mind with a distinct Chicago voice, words that make the city's neighborhoods spring to life, a flavor that stirs our imaginations with visions of characters walking Chicago's streets.

This gathering of short stories, personal essays and poems is by no means an all-encompassing anthology of Chicago literature. Such a work would require multiple volumes. However, this sampling does give the Chicago voice its due, and then some. Whether it's Stuart Dybek sharing his thoughts about a childhood field trip to Cook County Jail, Rick Kogan writing about the visitors to his parents' Old Town apartment, R.J. Eldridge painting the streets of Englewood with heart and soul, Patty McNair giving voice to a group of young girls coming to the big city from the burbs, or Gary Johnson bringing his Marquette Park neighborhood to life, circa 1976, the writers in this anthology speak a language we all know. Yes, they speak CHICAGOESE.

And that voice— it pounds, it pulsates, it oozes with city life. From Morgan Park to Humboldt Park, from the shores of Lake Michigan to the old Chicago stadium, from flea markets to barstools—the setting and writing style in each work are different, but what remains the same is that each story, personal essay and poem in this collection packs power and provokes thought. And each work in this book carries that one similarity that paved its way into this collection—its author speaks CHICAGOESE.

Bill Donlon and Dennis Foley, editors

We Speak CHICAGOESE

stories and poems by Chicago writers

STUART DYBEK

Field Trips

We took two field trips in grade school. The first was a tour of the Bridewell House of Corrections and the Cook County Jail. The prison complex was on 26th and California, only blocks away from St. Roman's school, so, herded by nuns into an orderly column with the girls in front and boys bringing up the rear, our fifth grade class walked there. The nuns must have thought it a perfect choice for a field trip as not only was there a suitable cautionary lesson, but it saved on bus fare, too.

Filing from school at midmorning felt like a jailbreak. Paired up with pals, we traipsed down California gaping like tourists at the familiar street coming to life — delivery trucks double parking before greasy spoons, open doors revealing the dark interiors of bars still exhaling boozy breath from the night before. Some of the kids like Bad Brad Norky — already twice convicted of stealing the class milk money — were hoping to see various relatives who were doing time at County. Others, like my best friend Rafael Mendoza, were hoping to catch a glimpse of a mob boss, or a mass murderer, or the infamous psychopath, Edward Gein, a farmer from the wilds of Illinois who supposedly cannibalized his victims and tanned their skins to make lampshades and clothes. Gein fascinated us. Some years later when I was in high school, I bought a pair of hand-stitched moccasin-top gray suede shoes that, when soaked with rain, turned a cadaverous shade, and my buddies took to calling them my Gein Shoes. That, in turn, developed into a neighborhood expression of appreciation for any article of clothing that looked sharp in an unconventional way: *muy Gein, man*, or *Gein cool!* At the same time, the term could also be used as an insult: "Your mama's a Gein."

Even more than the murderers and celebrity psychos, the main draw at County, at least for the boys, was getting a look at the electric chair. We'd heard it was kept in the basement. Local legend had it that a sudden burst of static on the radio or a blink in TV reception, say, during the *Howdy Doody Show*, meant that the power had surged because they'd just fried someone at County. We thought maybe we'd get to shake the hand of the warden or whoever flipped the switch at executions. But, if there was an electric-chair there at all, we never got to see it.

Surprisingly, the most memorable part of the trip occurred not at County where the men, penned in what the tour guide informed us were 60 square foot cells, mostly ignored us, but rather at Bridewell when they took us through the women's wing. The inmates there, prostitutes mainly, saw the nuns and had some comments about being Brides of Christ that were truly educational:

"Yo Sisters, what kinda meat do the Pope eat on Friday? Nun."

"Hey, Sister Mary Hymen, when I dress up like that I get an extra fifty!"

The nuns didn't respond, but their faces assumed the same impassive, inwardly suffering expressions that the statues of martyrs wore, and they began to hurry us through the rest of the tour.

A hefty female guard rapped the bars with her stick and shouted, "Pipe down, Taffy, there's kids for godssake."

And Taffy laughed, "Shee-it, Bull Moose! When I was their age I was doing my daddy."

And from another cell someone called, "Amen, girl!"

The next year the nuns avoided the jail and instead took us to the stockyards, a trip that required a bus. A rented yellow school bus was already waiting when we got to school that morning, and we filed on, boys sitting on the left side of the aisle, girls on the right. I sat next to a new kid, Joseph Bonnamo. Usually, new kids were quiet and withdrawn, but Bonnamo, who'd only been at St. Roman's for a couple weeks, was already the most popular boy in the class. Everyone called him Joey B. His father had been a Marine lifer and Joey B. was used to moving around, he said. He'd moved around so much that he was a grade behind, a year older than everyone else, but he didn't seem ashamed by it. He was a good athlete and the girls all had crushes on him. That included Sylvie Perez, who over the summer had suddenly, to use my mother's word, "developed." Exploded into bloom was closer to the truth. Along with the rest of the boys, I pretended as best I could not to

notice—it was too intimidating to those of us who'd
been her classmates for years. But not to Joey B.

"Like my old man says, 'Tits that size have a mind of
their own,'" he confided to me on the way to the Yards,
"and hers are thinking 'feel me up, Joey B.'"

"How do you know?"

His hand dropped down and he clutched his crotch.
"Telepathy."

"Class," Sister Bull Moose asked, "do you know our
tradition when riding a bus on a field trip?"

"A round pound?" Joey B. whispered to me.

No one raised a hand. We didn't know we had a
tradition—as far as we knew we were the first class from
St. Roman's ever to take a bus on a field trip.

Sister Bull Moose's real name was Sister Amabilia,
but she had a heft to her that meant business, and
wielded the baton she used to conduct choir practice not
unlike the guard we'd seen wielding a nightstick at
Bridewell a year before, so my friend Rafael had come
up with the nickname. From within her habit, a garment
that looked as if it had infinite storage capacity, she
produced the pitch pipe also used in choir practice and
sustained a note. "Girls start and boys come in on
'Merrily merrily merrily . . .'"

Joey B. sang in my ear, "Row row row your boner . . ."

At the Yards there was a regular tour. First stop was
the Armour packing plant where the meat was
processed into bacon and sausage. I think the entire class
was relieved that the smell wasn't as bad as we worried
it might be. We knew we had traveled to the source of
what in the neighborhood was called "the brown wind"

or "the glue pee-ew factory," a stench that settled over the south side of Chicago at least once a week. My father said it was the smell of boiling hooves, hair, and bone rendered down to make soap. I'd once dissected a bar of Ivory on which I'd noticed what appeared to be animal hair to see if there were also fragments of bone and if beneath the soap smell I could detect the reek of the Yards.

We left the processing plant for the slaughterhouse and from a metal catwalk looked upon the scene below where workmen wearing yellow hard hats and white coats smeared with gore heaved sledge hammers down on the skulls of the steers that, urged by electric prods, filed obediently through wooden chutes.

Every time the hammer connected, my friend, Rafael would go, "Ka-boom!"

The steer would drop folding at the knees as if it was his front legs that had suddenly been broken.

"That has to smart," Joey B. said.

For the finale they took us to where the hogs were slaughtered. A man with hairy, thick, spattered forearms, wearing rubber boots and a black rubber apron shiny with blood stood holding a butcher knife before a vat of water. An assembly line of huge, squealing hogs, suspended by their hind legs, swung past him, and as each hog went by the line would pause long enough for the man to slit the hog's throat. He did it with a practiced, effortless motion and I wondered how long he'd had the job, what it had been like on his first day, and if it was a job I could ever be desperate enough to do. Up to then, my idea of the worst job one could have was bus driver. I didn't think I could drive through rush hour traffic down the same street over and over while making change as bus drivers had to in those days. But watching the man kill hogs, I began to think that driving a bus might not be so bad.

With each hog there was the same terrified squeal, but louder than a squeal, more like a shriek that became a grunting gurgle of blood. A Niagara of blood splashed to the tile and into a flowing gutter of water where it rushed frothing away. The man would plunge the knife into the vat of water before him and the water clouded pink, then he'd withdraw the shining blade just as the next squealing hog arrived. Meanwhile, the hogs who'd just cranked by, still alive, their mouths, nostrils, and slit throats pumping dark red gouts were swung into a bundle of hanging bodies to bleed. Each new carcass slammed into the others causing a few weak squeals and a fresh gush of blood.

The tour guide apologized that we couldn't see the sheep slaughtered. He said that some people thought the sheep sounded human, like children, and that bothered some people, so they didn't include it on the tour. It made me wonder who killed the sheep. We'd seen the men with sledgehammers and the man with a knife. How were the sheep slaughtered? Was it a promotion to work with the sheep—some place they sent only the most expert slaughterers—or was it the job that nobody at the Yards wanted?

"Just like the goddamn electric chair," Rafael complained.

"How's that?" Joey B. asked.

"They wouldn't let us see the chair when we went to the jail last year."

At the end of the tour on our way out of the processing plant they gave each of us a souvenir hot dog. Not a hot dog Chicago style: poppy seed bun, mustard—never catsup—onion, relish, tomato, pickle, peppers, celery salt. This was a cold hot dog wrapped in a napkin. We hadn't had lunch and everyone was starving. We rode back on the bus eating our hot dogs, while singing *"Frèrre Jacques."*

I was sitting by the window, Joey B. beside me and right across the aisle from him—no accident, probably— was Sylvie Perez. I realized it was a great opportunity, but I could never think of anything to say to girls in a situation like that.

"Sylvie," Joey said, "you liking that hot dog?"

"It's okay," Sylvie said.

"You look good eating it," he told her.

It sounded like the stupidest thing I'd ever heard, but all she did was blush, smile at him, and take another demure nibble.

I knew it was against the rules, but I cracked opened the window of the bus and tried to flick my balled up hot dog napkin into a passing convertible. Sister Bull Moose saw me do it.

"Why does there always have to be one who's not mature enough to take on trips?" she asked, rhetorically. For punishment I had to give up my seat and stand in the aisle which I did to an indifference on the part of Sylvie Perez that was the worst kind of scorn.

"Since you obviously need special attention, Stuart, you can sing us a round," Sister said. Once, during our weekly music hour, looking in my direction, she'd

inquired, "Who is singing like an off-key foghorn?"
When I'd shut up, still moving my mouth, but only
pretending to sing, she'd said, "that's better."

"I don't know the words," I said.

"Oh, I think you do. *Dor-mez-vous, dor-mez-vous, Bim
Bam Boon.* They're easy."

Joey B. patted the now empty seat beside him as if to
say to Sylvie, "Now you can sit here."

Sylvie rolled her pretty eyes toward Sister Bull Moose
and smiled, and Joey B. nodded he understood and
smiled back, and they rode like that in silence,
communicating telepathically while I sang.

RICK KOGAN

Typewriters

In the beginning was the sound and the sound was with me and the sound was the sound of a typewriter...a sound that accompanies my first memories.

I was born, I was told, at 3:30 a.m., a bit before what I would come to know as last call, on September 13, 1951 and in a couple of years was living in an apartment in Old Town, filled with the sound of the typewriter.

My father Herman wrote books.

He banged them out, two fingers pounding furiously, books about people with cartoon character names and events often bathed in blood.

He was a newspaperman in love with Chicago and its history. Vividly, often in collaboration with his newspaper pal Lloyd Wendt, my father wrote books about that history and among them are "Lords of the Levee," the story of First Ward bosses John "Bathhouse John" Coughlin and Michael "Hinky Dink" Kenna; "Give the Lady What She Wants," a history of Marshall Field & Co.; "Big Bill of Chicago," a biography of Mayor William Hale Thompson; and "Chicago: A Pictorial History."

He wrote almost all of these books in a small office at the front of our apartment.

So, I hear a typewriter and another sound too, the sound of parties in the living room. I am in the bedroom I share with my younger brother Mark and there we toss toward sleep knowing that sooner or later, sleeping or not, we will be roused from bed.

My mother would say, "Get up now. Get up and come say good night to all the nice people."

In pajamas covered with cowboys and Indians we walked down the hall and into a living room at once exotic, alluring and terrifying, a wild mix of people and conversations, ice cubes banging against glasses filled with booze and music pouring from the stereo, cigarette smoke filling the air like fog.

The faces that accompany this memory are many, for my parents had many friends and some of them were famous and some of them talented.

Sometimes I see James Jones, built like a boxer and the author of "From Here To Eternity," sleeping for a week on the living room couch. I see the dapper Willard Motley, whose novel "Knock On Any Door" had its hero Nick Romano saying one of fiction's most memorable lines ("Live fast, die young and have a good-looking corpse"), walking through the door and giving to my brother and me some silver coins he had brought us from Mexico.

There were many others: musician Win Stracke, mime Marcel Marceau, actress Nancy Kelly, radio's Studs Terkel, comedy's Mort Sahl...But most of the people who partied in that living room and, when the weather was agreeable, on the back porch, were writers.

The paperback edition of Nelson Algren's "Chicago: City on the Make" was published in 1961, a decade after it originally appeared in print in the October 1951 issue of Holiday magazine as a less-catchy "One Man's Chicago" and a few months later and longer in book form with its now familiar title.

The 1961 edition, which included a new introduction by the author and a handsome photo of him, was priced at 95 cents and was dedicated to my parents, "Herman and Marilou Kogan," though my mother was ever "Marilew."

It took me many years to understand the significant part that Nelson played in my family. It was not until I was in my teens that I started reading him. He was, by this mid-1960s time, just about done. His reputation was still sturdy, sitting on the foundation of "Somebody In Boots," "Never Come Morning," "The Man With the Golden Arm," and "A Walk on the Wild Side." But after 1956 he never wrote another novel. He turned out stories, poems, essays and journalism, many of them collected in "The Last Carousel" in 1973. But that was it. My father and Nelson's great pal and running buddy, the photographer Art Shay, once estimated that Algren's poker playing — "he was only a fair player but thought himself a master," said Art — cost the world of literature perhaps four great novels.

Art told me this many years ago: "Nelson blew a lot of books that we should have had. He blew them gambling and with dames. But what he wrote is a treasure."

He told me this in a most unlikely and dangerous place, standing exactly where Art says that Nelson shared the "squeaky bed" in his second floor apartment at 1523 West Wabansia with French novelist-philosopher Simone de Beauvoir. The place was dangerous because the apartment stood in what is now the right lane of the northbound Kennedy Expressway and Art wanted to take a picture there.

"I had a nude of Simone that didn't get in my latest book," he said. "It was too private to get published." Nelson's relationship with de Beauvoir was his most famous and ugly. But he had others. Most people forget, or never knew, that in 1937 he married Amanda Kontowicz. They divorced in 1946, remarried in 1953, divorced again in 1955. In 1965 he married an actress named Betty Bendyk. They divorced three years later. And somewhere during all this there was my aunt Ginny.

I learned of this one early afternoon in the early 1970s. I was driving a cab and had saved enough money to invite my aunt to lunch at the Wrigley Building restaurant. Virginia Cavanagh was my mother's older sister. We called her Ginny and by "we" I mean myself and Ty Bauler (Paddy's grandson), Johnny Pareskevas and some of the other kids I grew up with in Old Town. Ginny would often have us over for sleepovers at the apartment she rented on Lake Shore Drive. She would take us to movies and museums and restaurants. She would buy canvases and paints and take us to the lakefront and to parks and teach us how to paint, how to see, how to appreciate place. These adventures endeared Ginny to me in ways that deeply affected me at the time and still do.

I had not seen her in a while when I invited her to lunch but she looked just as my memory had her when she walked into the Wrigley Building restaurant.

We sat down and she said, "Do you have a girlfriend?"

"Yes," I said.

"Are you nice to her?"

"I think I am," I said.

"Are you nice to her after you fuck her?" she said.

Now, this was as shocking to me as if Ginny's hair had caught fire, especially since the word "fuck" was not spoken but shouted, almost a scream.

All I could say was, "What?"

"After you fuck her, are you nice?" she said, again shouting that one word.

"Ginny…," I said.

"You should be," she said. "You should be nice. Nelson Algren was not nice."

Algren was to me at the time a god, his words and characters shadowing all of my weak attempts at short story writing. The heaviest influence was his vision of and relationship with Chicago. I was drunk with the city and driving through its every corner day after day, and it was almost as if Nelson was sharing the front seat of my Checker cab.

And here was Ginny, making of this god-companion a man, and a bad one.

"After he would fuck me, he didn't say a word," she said, again screaming that one word.

Marco, the Wrigley Building maitre d' and a man of impeccable manners and great understanding in the era of the three martini lunch, walked to the table.

"Mr. Kogan," he whispered in my ear (he was also a man of formality), as Ginny kept talking and yelling that word, "Please, your aunt is a nice lady but she has got to stop screaming. The other people are all looking. I think you will have to leave."

They were looking, some of them even laughing. I felt bad for Ginny, object of such cruel curiosity. "This place is too expensive," I said to her. "Let's go down to Riccardo's."

And we did, to the bar/restaurant where my parents had met many years before, and where Nelson had taken Ginny on a couple of dates, which she began to detail.

"Ginny," I said, pleadingly. "Let's talk about something, someone else."

"You're right," she said. There was a sadness in her voice and eyes. "Just this then. He was a beast to women and I think he slept with me because he couldn't have your mother. She was lucky."

"Now we really do have to talk about something else," I said.

And we did. Indeed, we never again talked about Nelson and I only saw him once more before he bid his bitter farewell to Chicago in 1975.

I was walking down State near Pearson when I saw him walking toward me. It was late, or early, depending on one's habits: 2 a.m. He was wearing a raggedy Army jacket and had the look, as Studs once put it, "of a horse player who just got the news: he had bet her across the board and she came in a strong fourth."

I stopped him and introduced myself.

"Little Rick," he said, obviously surprised.

We talked on the sidewalk for a while. He asked about my parents. I asked about his work.

"You used to know my aunt," I said.

"Ginny? That aunt?" he said. "I knew her. She was a little crazy."

"Fuck you," I said and walked away.

Ginny died in 1987 in Chicago. Nelson died in 1981 in Sag Harbor, N.Y. They both died alone, perhaps lonely. But they are now forever linked in my memory. There is no sound attached, no typewriter and no ice cubes against glass. But I see them dancing. I see them happy and I know this because they are smiling.

JOHN GUZLOWSKI

Looking for Work in America

1. What he brought with him
He knew death the way a blind man
knows his mother's voice. He had walked
through villages in Poland and Germany

where only the old were left to search
for oats in the fields or beg the soldiers
for a cup of milk. He knew the dead,

the way they smelled and their dark full faces,
the clack of their teeth when they were desperate
to tell you of their lives. Once he watched

a woman in the moments before she died
take a stick and try to write her name
in the mud where she lay. He'd buried

children too, and he knew he could do any kind
of work a man could ask him to do.
He knew there was only work or death.

He could dig up beets and drag fallen trees
without bread or hope. The war taught him how.
He came to the States with this and his tools,

hands that had worked bricks and frozen mud
and knew the language the shit bosses spoke.

**2. I Dream of My Father as He Was When He
First Came Here Looking for Work**
I wake up at the Greyhound Station
in Chicago, and my father stands there,
strong and brave, the young man of my poems,
a man who can eat bark and take a blow
to the head and ask you if you have more.

In each hand he holds a wooden suitcase
and I ask him if they are heavy.

He smiles, "Well, yes, naturally. They're made
of wood," but he doesn't put them down.
Then he tells me he has come from the war
but remembers little, only one story:

Somewhere in a gray garden he once watched
a German sergeant chop a chicken up
for soup and place the pieces in a pot,
everything, even the head and meatless feet.
Then he ate all the soup and wrapped the bones
in cloth for later. My father tells me,
"Remember this: this is what war is.

One man has a chicken, and another doesn't.
One man is hungry and another isn't.
One man is alive and another is dead."

I say, there must be more, and he says,
"No, that's all there is. Everything else
is the fancy clothes they put on the corpse."

3.   His First Job in America

That first winter
working construction
west of Chicago
he loved the houses,
how fragile they looked,
the walls made of thin layers
of brick, the floors
just a single planking
of plywood.

A fussy, sleepy child
could destroy such a home.
It wasn't meant to witness
bombing or the work of snipers
or German 88s.

He worked there
until the cold and wind
cut him, and he found himself
thinking for hours of the way
he stacked bricks in the ruins
of Magdeburg and Berlin.

Finally, he quit
not because he was afraid
but because he knew
he could without fear

his shovel left
standing at an angle
in a pile of sand.

PATRICIA ANN McNAIR

Back to the Water's Edge

My girlfriends always drove because they had cars, cool cars: a Monte Carlo, a Cadillac, and best of all, the Trans Am. Boy bait. And that's what we were there for, after all, the boys. That, and a place that seemed about as far away as we could get from our land-locked suburban neighborhoods with low-slung ranch houses and two-car garages and flat, trimmed lawns.

Foster Beach.

The City. (You could hear how we capitalized it in the way we said it, like a title, a proper noun. The City. The City. THE CITY.)

The lake was there (*is* there), wide and wild sometimes, water rolling and crashing. Wild like we wanted to be, pulled by the moon on warm summer nights. And The City twinkled in the high rises behind us while we stood at the water's edge.

Mostly, though, we parked. All of us. We drove to the beach as though called there, a line of cars cruising slowly, looking for a spot in the lot where we could pull in and hop out and jump onto the hoods of our rides, onto the trunks. We sat in the humid dark while our warm engines ticked and cooled beneath us.

The seventies. And we were white girls from the suburbs grown bored with the white suburban boys we knew who were either jocks or freaks, and who had curfews and homework: read *The Canterbury Tales*, "The Knight's Tale;" solve for X, for Y; write a five-page paper on The Industrial Revolution.

My girlfriends, most of them, would drop out of high school, and I would go on to college, first one, then another, until I found the right one and made it work (Columbia College Chicago, just a few miles away from Foster Beach and overlooking that same great lake and the water's edge there.)

But we didn't know any of that yet.

What we knew was this: boys with names like Mario, like Ramon—City Boys—pulled huge speakers out of the trunks of their cars, played salsa at full volume, slapped their thighs and the vinyl landau tops in Latin rhythms. Clouds skittered across the moon lifting up over the water, and sometimes we would climb into the back seats of the cars with Mario, with Ramon, because they told us we were pretty. Different. And better times we would walk with them, holding hands and carrying our shoes, our toes in the sand close to the water's edge. And Mario, Ramon, would say "Let's sit, *sientate*," and we would, and the world (or maybe just the sand) would shift under our bodies. And we'd listen to the sometimes loud, sometimes quiet lap of water on land, to the music swinging through the night from the parking lot, to the cars behind us rushing along Lake Shore Drive, toward The City, or toward Hollywood at the Drive's end.

And sometimes, too, we'd lie back with Mario, with Ramon, and kiss under the summer stars that we couldn't really see because dark is never full dark in The City; there's always light. But we knew the stars were there like we knew other things: we were young. We were pretty (Mario said so, Ramon did.) We were miles away from home, from the suburbs, from sidewalks and shopping centers and our parents, asleep, probably, certain we were close by, safe, doing homework and sleeping over in twin beds in air-conditioned rooms. And we knew best of all that we would come back to this place, this City place, this Foster Beach. We would leave by the backdoors of our houses and tiptoe over the patios of our yards and meet at the stop sign, the Trans Am purring, the girls inside lipsticked and ready and eager to get there. Not just the next night, and the next, but always. We would return. Pulled (even now, forty years later) by the moon, by the boys and the music, by the cars and the parking, by the possibilities, by the memories.

Pulled again and again. Pulled back to the beach, back to the water's edge.

JOE MENO

Absolute Beginners

Nineteen-years old — I move in with a girl who I've
known for less than a year. We are students. The girl is
tall, blonde, and a whole lot smarter than me. We rent
the only place we can afford — a dingy, gray, stucco one-
bedroom affair in a low-income housing building in
Edgewater Beach. We live in a pair of dim rooms on the
nineteenth floor and pay four hundred bucks to the
Serbian landlords every month. One week after we
move in, we find a used syringe, lying in the hallway.
We decide to walk past it quickly. Down the hall, we
notice a sign has been taped to our neighbor's front
door. It says, "The drug dealers don't live here
anymore." People still show up at all hours and knock,
trying their luck. We just turn our radio up. One night, I
hear something crying in the stairwell, and go out to
find three mice, still alive — stuck in a glue trap. The
sound they make as they struggle to escape is the exact
sound of the way we imagine everyone feels living in
that building.

These young lovers do not do so well in the
summer months. When summer comes, the heat makes
the two rooms feel smaller than they actually are. We

argue about how often I am using drugs. Our fights get interrupted by the sound of other couples arguing. We can't compete with the way these other people howl, wail, and smash things that have been bought at the lousy dollar stores on our street. We cannot afford an air-conditioner, so we sit around in our underwear, listening to the sounds of other lovers breaking up.

Which is when we discover the lake. It has been here all this time, but it has been too cold and we have been too busy working at bad restaurants and going to school to notice. Each afternoon of that summer, we walk down to the lakefront, hurrying past Sheridan: we tread our way along the dark gray rocks, and in the midst of a number of sad-faced apartment buildings, old high-rises that, like their wrinkled inhabitants, have seen better days, we discover a secret. There is a beach here, in the middle of all this distress, in the middle of all this urban gloominess, right off of Thorndale Avenue, the great blue and gray and gold lake, a small stretch of white and yellow sand, with a few rocks to lay on—perfect for when the water gets too cold and you want to lie down and dry off and maybe try and hold hands. The elderly residents of these old high-rises, in loud cabana shirts and beige shorts, wearing black socks and brown sandals, stroll out from their buildings and sit on the benches, staring off at the enormity of the lake. Once or twice, we see a couple, a man and his wife, octogenarians for sure, whispering to each other, sharing a sandwich. We stare at them, at the lake, at our awful apartment building in the distance, and then at each other, and realize we are absolute amateurs at almost everything.

JOHN McNALLY

Working Stiff

"It is about ulcers as well as accidents, about shouting matches as well as fistfights, about nervous breakdowns as well as kicking the dog around. It is, above all (or beneath all), about daily humiliations." -- Studs Terkel, *Working*

I started working when I was six.

My father had taken me to a flea market to help sell some of his crap, and I gathered together some of my own crap to sell, including a large yellow toy dump truck. The flea market took place on the dusty gravel parking lot of a drive-in movie theater. While my father was busy talking to a customer at the other end of the table, a mother with a small child stepped up to examine our goods. The child, who was at least three years younger than me, started playing with the truck, so I cleared my throat, ready to yell out the toy's price in case either one asked me. Before I could say anything, however, they walked away. To my horror, the child took my dump truck with him.

At first I assumed that the mother didn't know what her horrible thieving spawn had done, but when she looked down at him and then back at me, who was glaring but not saying anything, I understood that the mother was complicit. They were a team, like Bonnie and Clyde, but instead of being lovers, as they were in the movie I had seen at the very drive-in I now stood in, they were mother and son.

Not only did I not make any money that day, but I was six years old and in the hole, where I would remain pretty much the rest of my life.

*

Despite this setback, I continued selling junk with my father at the flea market. I also supplemented my income whenever an opportunity arose, like those times my father offered a quarter for each pimple I popped on his back. This proved to be a short-term occupation since my father's back was vexed with hideous pimples for only a short period, but as a seven-year-old, I saw nothing disgusting or unusual about my task. On a good day, I might walk away with a five dollar bill. All profit.

But my primary income remained selling crap. After a few brutal Chicago winters that involved selling at indoor flea markets where we'd lug boxes across treacherous, icy parking lots in sub-zero weather, I negotiated a flat fee with my father rather than continuing to sell off my own toys. In exchange for my services, I would receive five dollars per work day – a respectable salary in 1975 for a nine-year-old.

That same year, we had moved from an apartment into a condominium, and in order to feed my record-buying appetite, I went door to door and offered my dog walking services to my new neighbors for the very reasonable fee of five dollars a week. I secured two clients, which brought my weekly salary up to twenty dollars, my monthly up to eighty.

Weekdays, I walked Ralph and Moo. Weekends, I sold crap at flea markets. I had come to realize that my father paid me not so much for my help but so that I could be a captive audience for his monologues that would go on for hours and hours. They were sometimes about what kinds of things he might buy wholesale to sell, or they were about how he was going to renovate a bread delivery truck into a walk-in store, complete with shelves full of merchandise.

These soliloquies drove me to the point where I considered opening the door of the van and jumping out while it was moving at sixty miles an hour. I couldn't bear listening to them. The van didn't have a passenger seat, so I sat on the floor, unbuckled, and leaned against a sheet of plywood that separated the front of the van from the back. I would sit there and wonder if the locked door would come unlocked if I pulled the handle. If so, I would roll out onto the side the road. For the duration of the drive, which was often two hours or longer, I would weigh the benefits against the disadvantages of going through with my plan. The whole while, my father would continue talking, every so often saying, "Huh? You say something?"

"No, Dad. I didn't say anything."

"Hunh? What was that?"

"I DIDN'T SAY ANYTHING!"

"Okay, goddamn it. Watch your tone. I'm your father, in case you forgot."

Once, I brought along a copy of *Mad Magazine* to read on the drive, but I had no sooner opened it up when my father said, "Fine. I guess I'm boring you. *Don't* listen to me then."

I lied. I said, "You're not boring me, Dad."

"Then why the hell aren't you listening?"

I looked at the door handle. More than ever before, I wanted to pull that handle, open the door, and jump out. I wanted to roll into a ditch and start running. But I was too much of a coward to go through with it, which is a good thing, since I would likely have died upon impact.

Another time, I brought a cassette player to the flea market so I could at least listen to music while we sat in the drive-in's dusty parking lot. I needed it to drown out my father's voice. But shortly after I pressed the play button, my father said, "Turn that down, for Christ's sake."

I turned it down. During a drum-heavy moment in the song, I started playing the air drums.

My father glanced over at me with an expression I had never seen before. The next time he glanced over, he said, "Stop doing that. It's embarrassing."

I was ten. My eyes grew warm, but I didn't cry. Embarrassing, I thought. I was embarrassing.

I turned off the music and refused to look at my father the rest of the day. This was the best punishment I could dole out, but it was lost on my father who launched back into one of his brain-numbing soliloquies, as though he hadn't, mere minutes earlier, crushed his son with a look of disgust and a single word.

*

The money I was making wasn't enough.

And so in the seventh grade I started making

bootleg cassettes and 8-tracks of newly released albums, and I sold them to my classmates. The reason why the tapes lacked a label or any artwork (I explained to anyone interested) was because I had a cousin who worked at Columbia House in Indiana, and they were fresh off the assembly line.

"You want to pay five dollars at a record store?" I asked. "Or do you want to pay me a dollar for the same thing? You decide."

My record collection was such that I could offer a comprehensive selection, but after I delivered the first few tapes, my unhappy customers cried foul and wanted a refund.

"You made these yourself!" one of them said.

"This is *your* writing on these," someone else said. "You don't have a cousin at Columbia House!"

I tried arguing my case, but it was futile, so I offered refunds to any dissatisfied customers, which turned out to be all of them.

A few weeks later, I began selling knives to my classmates. Not just any kind of knife. These were menacing knives with dragons on their handles and blades six inches long. My father had bought several dozen for us to sell at the flea market, some of which were practical, like the one for scaling fish, and some of which weren't, like the one whose handle had contours to accommodate a clenched fist. Under the guise of building up my own knife collection, I bought several from my father at wholesale prices and then took them to school to sell at a significant mark-up. I sold a few to boys who were top candidates for murdering me after school, but I didn't care. It was money in my pocket. But before I could sell any more, a teacher saw me flashing a blade on the blacktop before school one morning.

"It's just a knife," I said.

"Hand it over," he said. It was a teacher who knew me but didn't particularly like me because I was a fat kid. He favored the popular kids, not the outcasts or the troublemakers. "Why did you bring this to school?"

"To show a friend," I said.

"Is that all?" he asked. "To show a friend?"

I nodded.

He gave the knife back to me. "Don't bring it back," he said, "or I'll have to take it away."

I nodded again. I put the knife in the front pocket of my Huskies, where it remained for the rest of the school day.

Later that night, I sat in my bedroom, strategizing. I still needed more money, and I still had all these knives I needed to move. I took the knife out of my pocket and practiced flicking it open. The flick was successful only when I heard the lock snap into place. To close the knife, I had to depress the lock with my right thumb while closing the blade with my left hand. I repeated this action, over and over, all the while considering my options – sell the knives after school? sell them before school? – when the blade got stuck and wouldn't shut.

I pushed the blade harder, but it barely budged. I looked down to see what the problem was, and here's what I saw: half of my forefinger was on one side of the blade while the other half was on the other half of the blade. I had cut my finger in half from the top down.

Two observations:

1) When a knife is extraordinarily sharp, you don't immediately feel pain.

2) A swift, deep cut doesn't bleed right away.

As soon as I removed the knife, my finger began throbbing, and blood pumped out at a startling rate.

At the hospital, I told doctors and nurses that I had cut my fingers while slicing open a watermelon. No one believed me, but I stuck to my story so that there was nothing they could do to my parents. I was protecting them. The watermelon story was the best I could come up with. I loved watermelon, after all, and I had recently sliced one open, so there was the ring of truth to it, even though it was unlikely, if not impossible, that I would have cut open my finger doing what I had described.

A doctor stitched my finger back together and I was released, but the tip of my finger would have no feeling for decades, a constant reminder never to get too enamored with the things that were meant to generate income.

I sold my remaining knives back to my father, who sold them at the flea market, and with my forefinger bandaged in such a way that it looked like a cartoon appendage, I decided to leave the weapons business for good.

*

With the exception of a brief attempt to run his own rug cleaning business, my father was a roofer. He belonged to the roofer's union. He worked with hot tar, mostly. Flat roofs. He started in his teens and took an early retirement shortly after my mother died. All told, he was a roofer for over thirty years.

My father rarely made friends with the men from work, but when I was in the sixth grade, my father, mother, and I went to the house of a man named Larry Hunter. In addition to being a roofer, Larry Hunter was an Amway salesman, and the reason we went to his house was to attend an Amway recruitment meeting. My father's idea of the American Dream was to make a killing, as he'd have put it, and so he was eager to go to the meeting. Amway, which had long been accused of being a pyramid scheme and was a few years shy of being found guilty of price-fixing and making exaggerated income claims, produced a variety of cleaning products for their salesforce to sell at their places of work, to relatives and friends, or door-to-door, all while recruiting more salesmen and saleswomen.

Larry Hunter's daughters tried to wrangle me into playing a board game with them during the presentation. It would always be a difficult decision for me, deciding which one to follow – girls or money – but that day I followed neither. I followed the weirdness. Weirdness was a powerful pull, and there was no shortage of it that evening in Larry Hunter's living room. Even as a child, standing on the sidelines, I felt the slimy cultishness of Amway as Larry Hunter delivered his speech to a roomful of men and women wearing loud, ill-fitting clothes.

A month later, my father – now a part-time Amway salesman – wasn't seeing the vast profits he'd envisioned while at Larry Hunter's house. This was the promise of failure that I would see repeated throughout my father's life. At the start of each venture – window repair, leather and vinyl repair, gold plating – my father would get a look in his eyes like that of a gambler in an old movie whose face would be superimposed over dollar signs as he drives into Vegas, but only a short while later that look would change to disappointment and then anger, and he would refuse to talk about the failed business.

Six months after the Amway meeting, my father came home from work early, looking unnerved in a way I had never seen before.

His hands were shaking as he lit a Lucky Strike. "That son of a bitch tried to throw me off the roof," he said.

"Who?"

"Hunter," my father said. "He came to work drunk and wanted to fight. And then he tried throwing me off the goddamn roof."

According to my father, some of the other men restrained Larry Hunter so that my father could climb down the ladder. Once on solid ground, my father quit his job and drove to the union hall to put his name in the book. This was what you did when you needed a new job: put your name in the book and waited your turn.

My father stuck to his story that Larry Hunter was drunk, that he was a crazy son of a bitch, but the story never added up for me. Did my father owe him money for Amway products he hadn't sold? Or had my father provoked him? My father wouldn't have hesitated calling him a lying cocksucker to his face, and Larry might have reacted in a way that my father had not expected. I, too, sometimes blurted out insults on the playground, only to realize I'd royally screwed up once the aggrieved party's friends surrounded me later that night on their 3-speed Huffys.

Years later, my father and Larry Hunter's path crossed again at a flea market. We were manning our table, and even though years had passed and I had met Larry Hunter only once, I recognized him immediately.

Larry, squinting, approached our table. "Bob? Is that you?"

At the sight of Larry, my father's entire composure changed, like a cornered animal in the wild.

Even as a teenager I was good at reading people, picking up the subtext in a glance or a word, but on that day I saw nothing in Larry Hunter's behavior that suggested that he had once tried to kill my father. In fact, he seemed confused by my father's monosyllabic answers and grunts, by his disinterest to engage.

"Well then," Larry said before walking away. "Good seeing you, Bob. You take care of yourself, you hear?"

My father grunted. Once Larry was out of earshot, my father turned to me and said, "That's the cocksucker who tried pushing me off the roof."

"I know," I said.

I had seen teachers physically abuse students, and I had seen students assault other students, and now I realized that it would be no different once I started a real job.

I would never learn the truth of what happened between my father and Larry Hunter, or if *anything* had happened to prompt Larry Hunter to do what he had done, but I had never seen my father as frightened as I did that day.

"Let's pack up and get the hell out of here," my father said, trying to see which direction Larry Hunter had gone. "Fuck it," he added, tossing our merchandise, even things that were fragile, into boxes without any regard for order.

I didn't argue in favor of staying. I helped my father pack, and in a matter of just a few minutes, we got the hell out of there.

*

The summer between eighth grade and high school, I was offered a three-day gig to be Big Bird for a local car dealership. At six dollars an hour, I would be paid $144 in cash, and no one would be the wiser.

I had already gotten a raise walking dogs, and I still helped my father at the flea market. My total earnings for that month were close to $300, the equivalent of almost $1,000 today.

The Big Bird job was not without problems. The feathered suit was extraordinarily hot in July. The days were long with few breaks. A high percentage of passengers in passing cars either flipped me off or threw garbage at me. To add insult to injury, the costume didn't really look like Big Bird. Granted, I was a bird that was big, but Big Bird I was not. And kids who had come to see Big Bird told me so.

"Your beak doesn't even move," one kid said, and another kid noted with disgust that I sounded nothing like his beloved fictional character.

The benefits outweighed the disadvantages when it came time to take photos with customers. How many cute teenage girls and attractive young mothers sat on my lap? Pretty much everything gave me a boner back then, and if not for the thick, feathered suit, these poor girls and women would have felt Big Bird's weenie pressing against them. Fortunately, they didn't know that inside the costume was a horny, prepubescent boy grunting softly through the screen inside the bird's open beak, and that he wanted to dry hump each and every one of them. For this, I was getting paid handsomely. But it was over in three days, and I was back to the slog of my regular routine, waiting for the next big thing to happen.

*

What I had thought would be the next big thing was a book I had spent two years writing and had finally finished the summer between eighth grade and high school. It was a nonfiction book about old time comedians – Abbott and Costello, the Three Stooges, Laurel and Hardy, Charlie Chaplin, among others – and I had worked diligently on it, certain that a publisher would snap it up. I had written to publishers, who sent me information about their royalty rates, so I calculated how many books I would need in order to buy my parents a house. I had also written to any living actor or director who'd had any association with the comedians, and several wrote back to me, including Margaret Hamilton, most famous for playing the Wicked Witch of the West but who also appeared in a fairly awful Abbott and Costello movie. I wrote to authors for advice. I wrote to movie studios for information about reprinting photos. I wrote to memorabilia shops in Hollywood to ask for price-lists for movie stills. Every day, my parents' mailbox overflowed with letters from long-forgotten movie stars, movie studio legal departments, and fellow writers.

When it came time to submit the book, I closely followed the guidelines for sending query letters to publishers. I sent queries to every publisher in New York as well as a few in Illinois, as a backup. It didn't take long before rejections filled the mailbox, each one saying the same thing, that they didn't accept unsolicited manuscripts. How could this have been? What the hell?

By the end of summer, the book's fate had been sealed, and for a week after that realization, I brooded. But then I started another book. And then another. And then another. And then another.

Twenty-one years after that summer, my first book was finally published, proof that I am nothing if not persistent.

*

The big score did finally come for me and my father. It came in 1980 when I suggested that we sell concert t-shirts at the flea market instead of the turquoise and coral jewelry we'd been selling the previous few years. At my suggestion, my father found a guy who found a guy who knew a guy who illegally printed concert t-shirts, and we met the third guy in a parking lot behind McDonald's and bought fifty shirts in a variety of sizes featuring a variety of bands and singers: Bob Seger, Journey, REO Speedwagon, Triumph, etc. The usual.

The first time we took them to a flea market, we sold out.

My father bought several hundred more the next time, and, again, we sold out.

Over the next few years, we sold concert t-shirt and decorative feathers that hung from a strand of leather, at the end of which was a roach clip. We quit going to flea markets and traveled instead to city festivals. Corn Festivals. Apple Festivals. Harvest Days Festivals. We went to festivals in Illinois, Michigan, Indiana, and Wisconsin. The entire time, my father never quit talking, even when he'd wake me up at four a.m. so that we could get a prime spot to sell our shirts. And once we were set up, we couldn't keep the shirts in stock. People ate that shit up. But we were also met by religious conservatives in these small, far-flung towns, and they would berate us for promoting the devil's music.

"Hey!" my father would say, leaning across the table, getting in the man or woman's face. "No one's forcing you to buy one. So get the fuck away from our table." Once they were out of earshot, my father would turn to me and say, "Assholes." And then, "Fuck 'em."

*

It was not unusual for me to make a thousand dollars in a weekend. One weekend, we pulled in over three thousand dollars in sales. My pockets bulged with folded bills, and I had to be careful each time I reached in and yanked money out to give change so that the bills wouldn't fly away in a warm and gritty Midwestern wind that was as familiar to me growing up as snow in winter.

At our peak, I would personally profit anywhere from $500 to $1,000 for a single weekend of work. I would take my money to the mall during the week and burn through it all, mostly on albums and clothes. A cute girl with dark hair worked at J&R Music World, and I had hoped buying the entire back catalog of a band like The Police would impress her, so I would show up several times a week, carrying a pile of albums to the register for her to ring up. I would wear new clothes I'd bought at Chess King, maybe even a skinny tie like the kind Billy Joel wore at the time. But the girl, who was a few years older than me, was not impressed – not by my money, not by my musical tastes, and not by my clothes. Not by anything I did or said. Nothing worked. Nothing.

*

Here's what I knew about Barry: He lived in the small central Illinois town where my father and I had been going the previous five years for their annual festival. He had been a high school teacher but had been fired for reasons he only vaguely alluded to. A fling with several students' mothers who became jealous and vengeful, he told us once. He was in his thirties or forties, and he had, for reasons I couldn't fathom, befriended my father.

I didn't like Barry, but I couldn't quite put my finger on it at first. He came behind our table when he talked to us, which I didn't like at all. He stood too close. He met my eyes too often. I was, when I first met him, twelve years old and fat, but by our last encounter, I was sixteen and thin. Ever since I had begun losing weight, Barry would make note of how good I was looking.

"You have a girlfriend?" he'd ask, and when I'd shake my head, he'd say, "No? Why not?" He'd look me up and down, and then he'd meet my eyes again. To my father, he'd say, "You got a lady killer here," and then he'd put his hand on my back and let it linger too long.

"I don't like him," I told my father on several occasions.

"Why?"

"I don't like the way he looks at me."

"What the hell does that mean?"

And then I'd shake my head. My father had a blindspot whenever it came to men who gave him the least bit of their time. He was flattered. It stroked his ego. It didn't make a difference who they were or the nature of their character. If they gave him their ear, my father would in turn give them the benefit of the doubt.

"You know what?" he'd say. "You and your mother are just alike. Suspicious of everyone."

No, I thought. *Only those worthy of suspicion.*

The last year we went to Barry's town – the year I was sixteen – I had decided around lunchtime that I needed a break from my father, who wouldn't stop talking, so I walked to the McDonald's near the highway, several miles away. I walked for well over an hour, mostly on gravel roads with corn fields on either side of me. I walked until the road grew wider and turned from gravel to pavement. It was July, hotter than shit, but I didn't care. I listened to my Walkman all the way there, an Elton John cassette I had made for myself, an unofficial "best of." I walked and walked until I finally saw the golden arches.

I ordered my usual – a plain quarter pounder with cheese, a large fry, a Diet Coke, and a deep-fried apple pie – and then I sat down and took my sweet-ass time eating it. Being alone, eating my favorite food: this was bliss. I wanted to stay all day, but I couldn't. I knew my father was going to be pissed that I had been gone for so long, but so be it. I couldn't take it anymore – the same subjects, over and over, year after year, followed by, "What do you think?" My father hated whenever I was gone longer than he thought I should be gone, if only because he had to stand behind the table in silence. Not that he'd admit that this was the reason. But I knew. And so I braced myself when our table came back into view. What I didn't expect was Barry waiting beside my father, looking panicked.

"I drove all over looking for you," Barry said. "I'd have given you a ride."

"Where the hell have you been?" my father asked.

"McDonald's," I said.

"I checked McDonald's," Barry said. "I drove over there. Which way did you go?"

"I don't know," I said. "I walked past a lot of cornfields."

Barry looked confused. Then his eyes widened. "You walked to the *highway*?"

I nodded. Why was Barry even asking questions? Why was this of any concern to him?

Barry turned to my father. "That's four or five miles each way," he said. To me, he said, "You all right? You need some water?"

"I'm fine," I said.

I looked at my father, hoping he could see now how wrong this all was, but my father was still fuming about how long I had been gone. I turned back to Barry, who looked as though he'd missed his one opportunity to be alone with me, and he must have realized by the look I was giving him that it was too late now. I was onto him.

"We were worried about you," Barry said, but when he reached for my arm, I backed away. Even if my father couldn't see it, I knew that I had just avoided something awkward at best and dangerous at worst. And Barry knew I knew.

He walked around to the other side of the table and I never saw him again, but what disturbed me more was the fact that my father couldn't see what was so obviously wrong, how *I* was the one he was upset with and not this stranger whose own sketchy backstory didn't add up. For the rest of his life, I could never reconcile my father's blind willingness to trust a stranger over the more rational opinions of those closest to him.

*

As with most profitable enterprises, a rift occurred in the upper management – in this case, between me and my father. We had been partners for eleven years at this point, nearly all of my life, and we had weathered several bad years with little profit, but now, finally, we were enjoying the fruits of our labor. Or we should have been, at least.

The problem was this. My father had taken to telling anyone who would listen that the idea to sell T-shirts had been his. "This was the best goddamn idea I ever had," he'd say.

The idea, of course, had been mine. I remembered clearly the idea coming to me during one of my high school classes after months of seeing my classmates wearing different black concert T-shirts day after day. These shirts were all some of my classmates ever wore. Sabbath. Rush. Zeppelin. The very day the idea came to me that this was what we should be selling, I told my father.

I was used to my father's revisionist histories, but I wasn't going to let him take credit for a suggestion that was now making us thousands of dollars each week. I couldn't let it slide.

And so I brought it up to my mother, who brought it up to my father, who denied that it had been my idea. He laughed it off.

"No, no," he said. "I remember when the idea came to me."

"What?" I yelled. "Are you kidding?"

"Hey! Watch your tone," my father said.

"But it was *my* idea," I said, a whine creeping into my voice.

My father yelled, "What the hell difference does it make?"

"What difference? You're telling everyone it was *your* idea. That's what difference it makes."

"Well," he said, getting angrier. "It *was* my idea."

I knew my father wasn't going to concede, so I left the house, my fists balled up, strange animal noises escaping from my throat. "*Gotttamnnnnitarghhhhhhhh.*" What I wanted was for my father to admit that all of his ideas had resulted in failure while my one idea, my *only* idea, was making us a small fortune, but I knew the man well enough to know that he had convinced himself that the idea really had been his. The memory of our conversation when I brought the idea to him? It was gone. Long fucking gone. Lost in the vast ocean of his own words and the sound of his own voice.

*

Around this time, we started seeing more competition. The competition, who were people we knew from the circuit who stole our idea, cut our profits in half. My father began driving us further and further away to escape the competition, which meant less sleep for me and longer monologues from my father.

Early one morning, while I was setting up a table, a young woman approached our table. She was holding her daughter's hand. The girl couldn't have been older than three. The top of her head barely reached the lip of the table. I was working alone. My father was busy chatting up one of the other sellers, probably buying whatever tall tale the seller was telling him. My father liked to believe that the other flea marketers were making lucrative livings by driving across the country in R.V.s and selling their shitty things. My father was gullible that way. If the subject was money, he believed whatever preposterous story anyone told him.

The mother standing at my table was pretty, and when she smiled at me, I smiled back. She stopped at the AC/DC T-shirt and read it aloud to her daughter.

"See what this says?" she said. "It says 'Highway to Hell.' And that's exactly where that man is going for selling these," she said, nodding toward me. "He's going to hell when he dies."

My hands began to shake. I was so angry, I felt like vomiting. I said, "If you're not going to buy anything, just move along."

Before walking away, she smiled at me in that self-satisfied way, as though to say, *See? You're not a nice boy at all.* And in that moment I wasn't a nice boy because I wanted to lean across the table and punch that woman. I wanted to knock that goddamn smile off her face.

It was that precise moment when I realized that I was done. I was done listening to people tell me that I was going to hell for selling stupid T-shirts. I was done listening to my father's monologues that went on for hours and hours. I was done waking up at ungodly hours, only to spend my weekends doing something I truly hated. The money was great, but the satisfaction of knowing it was over was greater. I felt relieved, much as I would feel relieved years later leaving other unpleasant jobs. The money wasn't enough. I hated what I was doing, but I hadn't realized just how much I hated it until I decided never to do it again.

I was so happy, I wanted to weep.

*

Not only did I never sell another thing at a flea market or town festival after that day, I didn't even go to a flea market or town festival for another twenty years. I would, of course, hold down any number of other jobs for periods as long as several years and as short as a day – movie theater usher, delivery man, shipping and receiving attendant, mall greeter, standardized test scorer, dormitory resident assistant. I even regularly sold plasma to make money. I did freelance writing and editing jobs. I threw parties and charged a cover. I did whatever I needed to do to stay afloat. And I also put myself in debt. Student loans. Credit cards. Personal loans. I couldn't dig myself out. I was in too deep. And so I worked, sometimes as many as three jobs at once: a full-time job, a part-time job at night, and temp work on the weekends. And even then I mostly managed just to scrape by.

Eleven years after I quit working with my father, I was a student in a Ph.D. program in English, and my father had driven to Nebraska to visit me. My father never gave a time-frame for how long his visits would last, and if I asked him, he would act as though he'd been insulted and leave, so his visits were always pressure cookers of tension and anxiety.

One afternoon, about a week into my father's visit, I had come home from a particularly frustrating day of teaching, and as soon as I stepped inside my suffocatingly small apartment, my father said, "How was your day?"

Instead of giving him a broad overview, I started talking about the fact that so few of my students could punctuate dialogue.

"Instead of putting the comma *inside* the quotation mark," I said, "they put it *outside*. Or they don't put one in at all. Or…"

My father stopped me. He said, "Why do you think I care about this? I'm not a writer. I don't know what the hell you're talking about."

And that was the moment. The pressure cooker exploded.

I said, "I don't expect you to know about this or care about it, but why the fuck do you think I'd have cared about anything you talked about all those years when we drove to flea markets? Why would a ten-year-old give a shit about measurements for boards you were going to cut or the truck you were going to buy or the sizes of engines or any of the shit you talked about? But did I ever say to you 'I don't care about this.' No! You know why? Because I was polite. But you know what? I *didn't* give a shit. About any of it! So the least you could have done was listen to me bitch about commas for ten fucking minutes."

As soon as I was done I realized I had stabbed my father through the heart and there was no taking it back. He was sixty-one that year, but he looked older as he sat there staring into his cup of coffee. He didn't have any money. His clothes were from Goodwill. All those years of work had amounted to nothing. What I had said was cruel, but it was too late to take any of it back.

"I'm sorry," he said, and though it wouldn't be the last time, it was the first time I remembered him apologizing to me for anything.

I sat down across from him that day in Nebraska. Whatever story he had told himself about the two of us, whatever grand and thrilling adventures he had remembered us having together, I had shattered it. And there was no putting it back together.

"Okay," I said to fill the void. "Okay."

*

My father died at eighty years old with only a few hundred dollars in his checking account, and he'd had that much only because he hadn't paid his bills before he died. He didn't have any belongings worth any money, and there was no savings account. Up until the very end, he'd say to me, whenever we spoke on the phone, "Boy, I'd love to see you hit it big one day. Wouldn't that be something!" Instead of filling me with optimism, my father's hope for me always made me despair.

I'm fifty years old as I write this. Twice divorced. Five cats. No kids. I live in Louisiana but have a house in North Carolina that I can't sell. And student loans. Good lord, those student loans. Each month, the credit card bills come with balances slightly larger than the previous month's. But I have projects in the works – a few big ones that could turn my ledger from red to black, if only they'd come through. I'm a tenured professor. I consider supplementing my income by driving for Uber or selling my collection of first editions or opening up an account on eBay for selling everything in my home. But the truth is, I'm tired – too tired to embark on yet another money-making venture.

My idea of the American dream? To live in a small apartment in the city of my choice. To own nothing but a few of my favorite books, a handful of albums I most love, an adequate stereo to listen to them on, and a comfortable chair. To owe nobody anything. Not one goddamn thing. To die debt-free. That's the dream.

RJ ELDRIDGE

Englewood

cop dog. drug mule.
gray streets. stole youth.
sore thumbs. blunt force.
your name: shift course.

black boy. broke home.
bad blood. dead dome.
gray streets. sharp stones.
dope fiends   die alone.

night fall. cold rain.
dry tear. wild brain.
green line. red line,
englewood. no time.

black lips. sore eyes.
stink swells. gut bites.
wet street. lockdown.
rahm say: *our town*

your way: bare lots,
sirens. gun shots.
southside boombox.
chief keef. black blocks.

gd!   lamron!
hellbent. hell song.
hellbound. hell home.
HELP US!
         none comes.

schoolhouse doors close.
food scarce. trees gone.
hair loss. swell gums.
infect blood-borne.

black boy. cold core.
feet hurt. soul sore.
your blocks. your score.
what you   cryin for?

SHERWOOD ANDERSON

Brothers

I am at my house in the country and it is late October.
It rains. Back of my house is a forest and in front there is
a road and beyond that open fields. The country is one
of low hills, flattening suddenly into plains. Some
twenty miles away, across the flat country, lies the huge
city Chicago.

On this rainy day the leaves of the trees that line the
road before my window are falling like rain, the yellow,
red and golden leaves fall straight down heavily. The
rain beats them brutally down. They are denied a last
golden flash across the sky. In October leaves should be
carried away, out over the plains, in a wind. They
should go dancing away.

Yesterday morning I arose at daybreak and went for a
walk. There was a heavy fog and I lost myself in it. I
went down into the plains and returned to the hills, and
everywhere the fog was as a wall before me. Out of it
trees sprang suddenly, grotesquely, as in a city street
late at night people come suddenly out of the darkness
into the circle of light under a street lamp. Above there
was the light of day forcing itself slowly into the fog.

The fog moved slowly. The tops of trees moved slowly. Under the trees the fog was dense, purple. It was like smoke lying in the streets of a factory town.

An old man came up to me in the fog. I know him well. The people here call him insane. "He is a little cracked," they say. He lives alone in a little house buried deep in the forest and has a small dog he carries always in his arms. On many mornings I have met him walking on the road and he has told me of men and women who are his brothers and sisters, his cousins, aunts, uncles, brothers-in-law. It is confusing. He cannot draw close to people near at hand so he gets hold of a name out of a newspaper and his mind plays with it. On one morning he told me he was a cousin to the man named Cox who at the time when I write is a candidate for the presidency. On another morning he told me that Caruso the singer had married a woman who was his sister-in-law. "She is my wife's sister," he said, holding the little dog close. His grey watery eyes looked appealing up to me. He wanted me to believe. "My wife was a sweet slim girl," he declared. "We lived together in a big house and in the morning walked about arm in arm. Now her sister has married Caruso the singer. He is of my family now." As someone had told me the old man had never married, I went away wondering. One morning in early September I came upon him sitting under a tree beside a path near his house. The dog barked at me and then ran and crept into his arms. At that time the Chicago newspapers were filled with the story of a millionaire who had got into trouble with his wife because of an intimacy with an actress. The old man told me that the actress was his sister. He is sixty years old and the actress whose story appeared in the newspapers is twenty but he spoke of their childhood together. "You would not realize it to see us now but we were poor then," he said. "It's true. We lived in a little house on the side of a hill. Once when there was a storm, the wind nearly swept our house away. How the wind blew! Our father was a carpenter and he built strong houses for other people but our own house he did not build very strong!" He shook his head sorrowfully. "My sister the actress has got into trouble. Our house is not built very strongly," he said as I went away along the path.

*   *   *   *   *

For a month, two months, the Chicago newspapers, that are delivered every morning in our village, have been filled with the story of a murder. A man there has murdered his wife and there seems no reason for the deed. The tale runs something like this--

The man, who is now on trial in the courts and will no doubt be hanged, worked in a bicycle factory where he was a foreman and lived with his wife and his wife's mother in an apartment on Thirty-second Street. He loved a girl who worked in the office of the factory where he was employed. She came from a town in Iowa and when she first came to the city lived with her aunt who has since died. To the foreman, a heavy stolid looking man with grey eyes, she seemed the most beautiful woman in the world. Her desk was by a window at an angle of the factory, a sort of wing of the building, and the foreman, down in the shop had a desk by another window. He sat at his desk making out sheets containing the record of the work done by each man in his department. When he looked up he could see the girl sitting at work at her desk. The notion got into his head that she was peculiarly lovely. He did not think of trying to draw close to her or of winning her love. He looked at her as one might look at a star or across a country of low hills in October when the leaves of the trees are all red and yellow gold. "She is a pure, virginal thing," he thought vaguely. "What can she be thinking about as she sits there by the window at work?"

In fancy the foreman took the girl from Iowa home with him to his apartment on Thirty-second Street and into the presence of his wife and his mother-in-law. All day in the shop and during the evening at home he carried her figure about with him in his mind. As he stood by a window in his apartment and looked out toward the Illinois Central railroad tracks and beyond the tracks to the lake, the girl was there beside him. Down below women walked in the street and in every woman he saw there was something of the Iowa girl. One woman walked as she did, another made a gesture with her hand that reminded of her. All the women he saw except his wife and his mother-in-law were like the girl he had taken inside himself.

The two women in his own house puzzled and confused him. They became suddenly unlovely and commonplace. His wife in particular was like some strange unlovely growth that had attached itself to his body.

In the evening after the day at the factory he went home to his own place and had dinner. He had always been a silent man and when he did not talk no one minded. After dinner he with his wife went to a picture show. There were two children and his wife expected another. They came into the apartment and sat down. The climb up two flights of stairs had wearied his wife. She sat in a chair beside her mother groaning with weariness.

The mother-in-law was the soul of goodness. She took the place of a servant in the home and got no pay. When her daughter wanted to go to a picture show she waved her hand and smiled. "Go on," she said. "I don't want to go. I'd rather sit here." She got a book and sat reading. The little boy of nine awoke and cried. He wanted to sit on the po-po. The mother-in-law attended to that.

After the man and his wife came home the three people sat in silence for an hour or two before bed time. The man pretended to read a newspaper. He looked at his hands. Although he had washed them carefully grease from the bicycle frames left dark stains under the nails. He thought of the Iowa girl and of her white quick hands playing over the keys of a typewriter. He felt dirty and uncomfortable.

The girl at the factory knew the foreman had fallen in love with her and the thought excited her a little. Since her aunt's death she had gone to live in a rooming house and had nothing to do in the evening. Although the foreman meant nothing to her she could in a way use him. To her he became a symbol. Sometimes he came into the office and stood for a moment by the door. His large hands were covered with black grease. She looked at him without seeing. In his place in her imagination stood a tall slender young man. Of the foreman she saw only the grey eyes that began to burn with a strange fire.

The eyes expressed eagerness, a humble and devout eagerness. In the presence of a man with such eyes she felt she need not be afraid.

She wanted a lover who would come to her with such a look in his eyes. Occasionally, perhaps once in two weeks, she stayed a little late at the office, pretending to have work that must be finished. Through the window she could see the foreman waiting. When everyone had gone she closed her desk and went into the street. At the same moment the foreman came out at the factory door. They walked together along the street a half dozen blocks to where she got aboard her car. The factory was in a place called South Chicago and as they went along evening was coming on. The streets were lined with small unpainted frame houses and dirty faced children ran screaming in the dusty roadway. They crossed over a bridge. Two abandoned coal barges lay rotting in the stream.

He went by her side walking heavily and striving to conceal his hands. He had scrubbed them carefully before leaving the factory but they seemed to him like heavy dirty pieces of waste matter hanging at his side. Their walking together happened but a few times and during one summer. "It's hot," he said. He never spoke to her of anything but the weather. "It's hot," he said. "I think it may rain."

She dreamed of the lover who would some time come, a tall fair young man, a rich man owning houses and lands. The workingman who walked beside her had nothing to do with her conception of love. She walked with him, stayed at the office until the others had gone to walk unobserved with him because of his eyes, because of the eager thing in his eyes that was at the same time humble, that bowed down to her. In his presence there was no danger, could be no danger. He would never attempt to approach too closely, to touch her with his hands. She was safe with him.

In his apartment in the evening the man sat under the electric light with his wife and his mother-in-law. In the next room his two children were asleep. In a short time his wife would have another child. He had been with her to a picture show and in a short time they would get into bed together.

He would lie awake thinking, would hear the creaking of the springs of a bed where, in another room, his mother-in-law was crawling between the sheets. Life was too intimate. He would lie awake eager, expectant -- expecting, what?

Nothing. Presently one of the children would cry. It wanted to get out of bed and sit on the po-po. Nothing strange or unusual or lovely would or could happen. Life was too close, intimate. Nothing that could happen in the apartment could in any way stir him; the things his wife might say, her occasional half-hearted outbursts of passion, the goodness of his mother-in-law who did the work of a servant without pay--

He sat in the apartment under the electric light pretending to read a newspaper--thinking. He looked at his hands. They were large, shapeless, a working-man's hands.

The figure of the girl from Iowa walked about the room. With her he went out of the apartment and walked in silence through miles of streets. It was not necessary to say words. He walked with her by a sea, along the crest of a mountain. The night was clear and silent and the stars shone. She also was a star. It was not necessary to say words.

Her eyes were like stars and her lips were like soft hills rising out of dim, star lit plains. "She is unattainable, she is far off like the stars," he thought. "She is unattainable like the stars but unlike the stars she breathes, she lives, like myself she has being."

One evening, some six weeks ago, the man who worked as foreman in the bicycle factory killed his wife and he is now in the courts being tried for murder. Every day the newspapers are filled with the story. On the evening of the murder he had taken his wife as usual to a picture show and they started home at nine. In Thirty-second Street, at a corner near their apartment building, the figure of a man darted suddenly out of an alleyway and then darted back again. The incident may have put the idea of killing his wife into the man's head. They got to the entrance to the apartment building and stepped into a dark hallway. Then quite suddenly and apparently without thought the man took a knife out of his pocket. "Suppose that man who darted into the alleyway had intended to kill us," he thought. Opening the knife he whirled about and struck at his wife. He struck twice, a dozen times-- madly. There was a scream and his wife's body fell.

The janitor had neglected to light the gas in the lower hallway. Afterwards, the foreman, decided, that was the reason he did it, that and the fact that the dark slinking figure of a man darted out of an alleyway and then darted back again. "Surely," he told himself, "I could never have done it had the gas been lighted."

He stood in the hallway thinking. His wife was dead and with her had died her unborn child. There was a sound of doors opening in the apartments above. For several minutes nothing happened. His wife and her unborn child were dead--that was all.

He ran upstairs thinking quickly. In the darkness on the lower stairway he had put the knife back into his pocket and, as it turned out later, there was no blood on his hands or on his clothes. The knife he later washed carefully in the bathroom, when the excitement had died down a little. He told everyone the same story. "There has been a holdup," he explained. "A man came slinking out of an alleyway and followed me and my wife home. He followed us into the hallway of the building and there was no light. The janitor has neglected to light the gas." Well--there had been a struggle and in the darkness his wife had been killed. He could not tell how it had happened. "There was no light. The janitor has neglected to light the gas," he kept saying.

For a day or two they did not question him specially and he had time to get rid of the knife. He took a long walk and threw it away into the river in South Chicago where the two abandoned coal barges lay rotting under the bridge, the bridge he had crossed when on the summer evenings he walked to the street car with the girl who was virginal and pure, who was far off and unattainable, like a star and yet not like a star.

And then he was arrested and right away he confessed--told everything. He said he did not know why he killed his wife and was careful to say nothing of the girl at the office. The newspapers tried to discover the motive for the crime. They are still trying. Someone had seen him on the few evenings when he walked with the girl and she was dragged into the affair and had her picture printed in the papers. That has been annoying for her as of course she has been able to prove she had nothing to do with the man.

*   *   *   *   *

Yesterday morning a heavy fog lay over our village here at the edge of the city and I went for a long walk in the early morning. As I returned out of the lowlands into our hill country I met the old man whose family has so many and such strange ramifications. For a time he walked beside me holding the little dog in his arms. It was cold and the dog whined and shivered. In the fog the old man's face was indistinct. It moved slowly back and forth with the fog banks of the upper air and with the tops of trees. He spoke of the man who has killed his wife and whose name is being shouted in the pages of the city newspapers that come to our village each morning. As he walked beside me he launched into a long tale concerning a life he and his brother, who has now become a murderer, once lived together. "He is my brother," he said over and over, shaking his head. He seemed afraid I would not believe. There was a fact that must be established. "We were boys together that man and I," he began again. "You see we played together in a barn back of our father's house. Our father went away to sea in a ship. That is the way our names became confused. You understand that. We have different names, but we are brothers. We had the same father. We played together in a barn back of our father's house. For hours we lay together in the hay in the barn and it was warm there."

In the fog the slender body of the old man became like a little gnarled tree. Then it became a thing suspended in air. It swung back and forth like a body hanging on the gallows. The face beseeched me to believe the story the lips were trying to tell. In my mind everything concerning the relationship of men and women became confused, a muddle. The spirit of the man who had killed his wife came into the body of the little old man there by the roadside.

It was striving to tell me the story it would never be able to tell in the court room in the city, in the presence of the judge. The whole story of mankind's loneliness, of the effort to reach out to unattainable beauty tried to get itself expressed from the lips of a mumbling old man, crazed with loneliness, who stood by the side of a country road on a foggy morning holding a little dog in his arms.

The arms of the old man held the dog so closely that it began to whine with pain. A sort of convulsion shook his body. The soul seemed striving to wrench itself out of the body, to fly away through the fog, down across the plain to the city, to the singer, the politician, the millionaire, the murderer, to its brothers, cousins, sisters, down in the city. The intensity of the old man's desire was terrible and in sympathy my body began to tremble. His arms tightened about the body of the little dog so that it cried with pain. I stepped forward and tore the arms away and the dog fell to the ground and lay whining. No doubt it had been injured. Perhaps ribs had been crushed. The old man stared at the dog lying at his feet as in the hallway of the apartment building the worker from the bicycle factory had stared at his dead wife. "We are brothers," he said again. "We have different names but we are brothers. Our father you understand went off to sea."

*   *   *   *   *

I am sitting in my house in the country and it rains. Before my eyes the hills fall suddenly away and there are the flat plains and beyond the plains the city. An hour ago the old man of the house in the forest went past my door and the little dog was not with him. It may be that as we talked in the fog he crushed the life out of his companion. It may be that the dog like the workman's wife and her unborn child is now dead. The leaves of the trees that line the road before my window are falling like rain--the yellow, red and golden leaves fall straight down, heavily. The rain beats them brutally down. They are denied a last golden flash across the sky. In October leaves should be carried away, out over the plains, in a wind. They should go dancing away.

CARL RICHARDS

My Brother's Ass

My brother's ass had staples in it
which attached him to a bar stool
for hours upon end, staring
into the haze of the black and white tube
Sox hat on his head
downing his Old Styles.
He took Wednesdays off.
Said it was his day of rest.
He told my mother
he'd get a job and
stop drinking.
He told me
his job was drinking.
Always had money in his pocket.
Lawsuits pay good dough
for an arm amputated.
He never smoked.
Said it would shorten his life.
Sometimes
his ass stayed put for days on that stool
but he would leave eventually
like an unruly relative on holiday
and work
his maze through our neighborhood,
a smile on his face
stumbling occasionally
waving with his good hand
And saying 'Yellow'
To anyone who crossed
His well worn path.

CRIS MAZZA

They'll Shoot You

1988

President Reagan on Michael Dukakis's campaign for the presidency: "You know, if I listened to him long enough, I would be convinced that we're in an economic downturn, and that people are homeless, and people are going without food and medical attention, and that we've got to do something about the unemployed."

This decision should be as easy as resolving to avoid dangerous places. She's going to tell him about it tonight.

Cici watches Jeremy's eyes move across hockey statistics in the newspaper. His mother has told Jeremy, in private, that Cici could use some cute new clothes to wear instead of jeans. Jeremy told Cici later. He also told her his mother had informed him — as though it took her a day and a half to do the subtraction — that Cici was eleven years younger than him. His answer: "So?" He was mean to his mother. Cici told him that in private. He laughed. "She needs to be kept in line," he said. "She might want me to start visiting more often."

He has decided that they'll leave for the hockey game three hours early, eat at the place where two larger-than-life hotdog people — one a girl, the other a boy — stand on the roof, then go to the game, walk around the inside of the stadium looking at the souvenirs, try to sneak down close to the ice to watch the warm-up, then find their seats, after the game go to Greektown for gyros.

"That stadium's in a bad place," his mother has said, just a minute ago. "They'll shoot you down there."

Cici had looked at Jeremy and he grinned back at her. "They will," he said, "every time you go."

Now his mother says, "The roads are icy."

"Maybe we'll be killed skidding off an overpass and you won't have to put up with us another three days."

"Oh *you*."

Cici keeps looking at Jeremy because after three days she won't be able to look at him anymore for a long time. He sticks out his tongue or crosses his eyes or makes a wildman face or grins a manic grin or smiles gently, sadly. He has lovely hazel down-turned eyes and sweetly crooked front teeth.

Long before this visit, Jeremy had told Cici over the phone, "My mother cries easier than anyone I know, except you. The biggest difference is that she can also stop on a dime. She might say five sentences, the first one she's normal, the next two she's crying, the fourth and fifth she's perfectly normal again, just bossy as usual, as though nothing happened."

"What does she cry about?" Cici had asked.

"She misses my father, she wants to see me more often, she's worried that Glenda will kill me."

"Does she cry when she tells you not to get married again?"

"No, that's when she's bossy. She's bossy about 90% of the time."

Just before the first time Cici had to leave Jeremy in California for what was then her new job in Cincinnati, he'd suggested she get a new car for the long trip, strongly recommended it, advised it, called around and found the lowest price on the type of vehicle best suited for her needs, forced the dealer to get it in the color Cici wanted. Tears gathered in his eyes the morning she left, his nose red and slightly transparent. She would've reached to touch the tears beginning to run down his face, but he held her too close, put his chin over the top of her head. She knew he wouldn't shut his eyes but would keep staring over her head around his garage. That's where they were. Finally he'd whispered, "I guess you better go." That was over a year ago. Since then she's had to leave him again and again, after being together a week, a month, three weeks, a weekend, two months. This time it's just five days together — all five at his mother's condo in the Sauganash neighborhood in Chicago, two thousand miles east of his house in Del Mar and Cici's currently uninhabited apartment in San Diego; eight hundred miles northwest of her rented room in Cincinnati.

"All set for hotdogs, hockey and gyros?" Jeremy says. He already has one arm in his coat.

"It's hours early," his mother says, "you don't need to go yet."

"We'll take a drive." He turns his back on his mother, rolling his eyes for Cici's benefit.

"It's icy," his mother says. "You should listen to the traffic report. You should take a cab."

"I drive better than a cab driver."

The few times it snowed in Cincinnati while she was there, Jeremy reminded Cici over the phone to drive slowly and make every motion smoothly: turning, braking, accelerating, everything.

"Why is it icy?" Cici sighs. "It's supposed to be spring. It *must* be spring. It's the middle of March, so it's supposed to be spring."

"Welcome to Chicago, baby."

He lets his mother's Buick fishtail down the street on the ice while Cici squeals and grabs his arm and shrieks "No, don't," laughing. Just before the busy cross street, he purposely skids and slides almost sideways at the stop sign, opens the window and shouts "Free at last!"

Now Cici's position as a seasonal botanical consultant at the Cincinnati Zoo, March through November, will probably be eliminated. When she'd first described her job to him, he'd asked if they would ever send her into a lion's cage or the wolf enclosure or a bear's habitat to inventory the flora or check damage to trees. A certain smile, showing his eyeteeth, means he's joking. At a traffic signal, looking at a burned and boarded-up house, imagining it new with the trim painted and flowers in the window boxes, people on the front porch waving as holiday guests leave on July 4, Cici says, "They may offer me a full time position instead. Twelve months instead of nine. I'd be there year-round."

"What? When did you find that out?"

"Last week."

"Why didn't you tell me?"

"I'm sorry. I was thinking about what I'm going to do."

"So, what're you going to do?"

"I don't know."

"You sound like they offered you terminal cancer instead of a job."

"That's exactly what they offered me."

Over dinner, she tries to smile at him with her mouth full of hotdog, onions and relish, not knowing what it looks like since it feels like a grimace with a lump in her throat. Like cancer. When it grows, it makes her cry. When she cries, it gets bigger. "You look like you really needed this," he says.

"Yes, just fill me with carcinogens and preservatives, I'll live forever. You don't have to worry about me."

When she had thought she might get a bicycle to keep in Cincinnati, he'd said he would worry about her getting hit by a car. When she wanted to take horseback riding lessons in Kentucky — something to stimulate her senses when she was away from him, she'd said, only partly joking, the heavy scent of horse and hay, pastoral beauty of a Kentucky farm, the warm solid feel of something alive between her legs — he'd said he was afraid she'd fall or be kicked or bitten. That time he hadn't been smiling.

She doesn't cry until just minutes into the game when two players fight and one comes away bloody, sent to sit alone in the penalty box and wipe his blood on a used towel. "It's so stupid," she sobs, "they ought to be ashamed."

He laughs. "This place is sold out, and you're the only one crying."

"But the babes with big hair snapping their gum aren't *going* to cry."

Finally the player throws away the dirty towel and bursts out of the box.

"What should I do, Jeremy?"

"I don't know what to tell you." No longer laughing.

It is cold in the stadium. She keeps her coat on and hugs herself. She'd almost left her gloves in the car, glad now that Jeremy had suggested she take them along, just in case.

All the cars had been parked side-by-side and end-to-end, a solid mass. Those fans earliest out to the lot sit idling, blowing steam, until a space breaks in front or behind. Jeremy tries to slide across each frozen puddle that isn't already cracked or smashed, some no larger than the length of his shoe. His mother's white Buick is still surrounded. "Chicago cars," he says, pointing to two of the closest ones with rusted-out fenders, dinks and dents, hanging mufflers. He'd told Cici to wash her new car once a week, especially during winter in Cincinnati, because of the salt.

The motor running, the heater on, he says, "I wish we were going back to a motel instead."

"Or home," Cici says. "I mean .... San Diego."

"I know." Sometimes his voice is so gentle, her insides kink up.

Last month when she left San Diego to return to Cincinnati for her spring contract, he'd said, "It's kind of fun, think of it that way, you're important, you're the only one who can do what you do, so they have to bring you in several times a year."

"I'm not the only one."

"But think of it that way, it'll make it easier, they need you."

"What about you?"

"I'll be okay. You'll be okay. We'll be okay. And when you come home, you can find a different apartment, okay?"

"Why? I hate moving."

"I don't like your neighborhood. I'm worried about it. It's changing. There's all those robberies and shootings and gang activity less than half a mile away. I worry about you at night, sometimes. Aren't you scared to sleep there?"

"I sleep there, what, 10% of the year?"

"More than that."

He'd told her to tell repairmen and door-to-door salesmen that she's married but her husband isn't home at the moment. He wanted her to somehow imply to the landlord that she was married or that her boyfriend was there most of the time.

"Why?"

"You can't tell what they'll think or do if they know you're living there alone. And *never* tell anyone you work out of town half the year."

"It's more than half, Jeremy."

Something hits the window beside Cici, a dull thud like someone's elbow or head. The big backside of a man blocks the window for a second, then he gets into the car beside them. "Too bad we can't drive sideways" she says. But the car beside them doesn't move. The occupants get out again and sit on the hood, drinking beer.

"Don't look at them," Jeremy mutters, but the man on the car hood has begun gesturing, his voice coming through the windows as though he's far away, "C'mon, join us for a brew, wut's yer hurry?"

"I already smiled at him by accident," Cici says.

"Uh-oh. Why'd you do that?"

The owners of the car on their other side have arrived, two more young men, but they don't leave either, just sit on their car's hood and trunk, swinging their legs and kicking the sides of Jeremy's mother's Buick. The first two men are right up against Cici's window, pressing their faces there, kissing the glass, their lips smashed like the underside of snails or slugs. The other two shout greetings and toss beers to three more guys arriving from the stadium who go to the cars in front and behind. One sits on the hood of the Buick. The others lean against the Buick's white fenders.

"What's going on, did they plan this?" Cici asks.

"Probably, when they got here."

"Why us?"

"Maybe because of the car looking so new, and it's a fucking *Buick*. Maybe just random."

On either side, two guys are tossing opened beers back and forth. Large splotches splatter the window like vomit.

"Jeremy ...?" Cici kneels on the seat, her back to the window. "Maybe ... could I, maybe ... instead of a new apartment, maybe I could move in with you ... I mean, when they eliminate my part-year position. I'm not asking for a free ride, it could save us both, I'd pay rent to you. I'd find some kind of job, I have lab experience, or I could teach intro to Biology at night school, I'd landscape your house, work at a nursery, I could even be a gardener, mow people's lawns."

"What about the full time thing they offered?"

"That's only a maybe. But you know what it would mean."

"I know."

The car starts to rock. Two guys in front and two guys in back are pushing up and down like a railroad handcar. One guy is still riding the hood.

"Assholes," Jeremy says. He leans on the horn.

"Is there a security guard?"

"Are you kidding?"

The car continues rocking. One of the guys in back is standing on the trunk. "My mother would be dead by now," Jeremy says. "Or else she'd just be her bossy self and they'd leave." He pushes a button that sucks the radio antenna into the fender. "Look, Cici, you've got to do what's right and best for *you*, for your life. I don't want to sound like an insurance-company cliché, but you've got to be independent, plan for your future, decide what you really want to do that can also give you some security, and build your life toward it."

As Cici lowers her face to Jeremy's lap to dry her eyes on his leg, he hisses, "God, no, sit up, think what it looks like you're doing!"

"I didn't want to wipe my eyes, I didn't want them to think I'm crying because of *them*." But the car is suddenly still, all seven guys begin whooping and circling the Buick, pounding the windows with their palms, shouting, "Go for it, baby," "more, more, more!"

"Eat it raw," and "deep-throat it, sweetheart, farther, farther!"

"Jeremy, have you ever thought about it, us living together?"

"I don't know, I like it the way it is now."

"With me gone *months* at a time?"

"Not that part."

"Do you *want* me to take the full time job in Cincinnati?"

"What I want can't enter your decision."

"But I've told you what *I* want."

The voices from outside are suddenly sharper.

"Hey, watch it," Jeremy says, "is your foot touching the window button?"

All the guys are piled on Cici's side, three or four hands coming through the window which has cracked open. Cici shrieks and lurches away from Jeremy, both her hands on the window button, catching their palms and fingers in a vise or dull guillotine as the window strains to close itself, and their voices accelerate into painful howls, rough laughter, drunken shouts, "Let me in, you sweet bitch."

"Ow, goddamnit, I'll kill your boyfriend, I'll cut his balls off."

"Let's paaaar-tayyyyy!"

"Put the window down," Jeremy shouts, "Put it *down*," lunging across Cici for the window controls, "let them out, open it, *open it!*"

But Cici's thumbs are white, bent backwards against the button, the window's motor whining, the safety glass continuing to trap and hold the renegade fingers — still reaching for her while trying to pull back, perhaps becoming frantic, even panicked, but locked in place.

STUART DYBEK

Clothespins

I once hit clothespins
for the Chicago Cubs.
I'd go out after supper
when the wash was in
and collect clothespins
from under four stories
of clothesline.
A swing-and-a-miss
was a strike-out;
the garage roof, Willie Mays,
pounding his mitt
under a pop fly.
Bushes, a double,
off the fence, triple,
and over, home run.
The bleachers roared.
I was all they ever needed for the flag.
New records every game—
once, 10 homers in a row!
But sometimes I'd tag them
so hard they'd explode,
legs flying apart in midair,
pieces spinning crazily
in all directions.
Foul Ball! What else
could I call it?
The bat was real.

ERIC CHARLES MAY

A Secret's Life, Mrs. Motley of Parkland, Chicago

Because she was born and raised in that far South Side neighborhood, which is where she taught for her 40-year career with the Public Schools, and where she married her husband, and raised her only child, and buried the husband, and served as a prominent member of her church; because of all that, residents of Parkland thought they knew Mrs. Motley pretty well, with some people—old childhood pals, former classmates, nearby neighbors, members of her congregation—going as far as to say that they knew her *very* well; knew her like they knew their own blood kin, like they knew themselves.

One keen observer gave an excellent physical description of her: "Tallish with a body that kinder neighborhood souls called slender and harder hearts labeled as bony, she had a skin tone the color of butterscotch and a head of silvery white hair combed back in a tight bun..." The observer goes on to say that everyday, Mrs. Motley wore dress blouses, skirts, and low-heel shoes "...as if important company was coming or she had someplace important to go." Along with clear, manicured fingernails, she wore round wire-rim glasses that the observer says, "...were set low on her long nose..." In addition, she was sober, never spoke loudly, and never cursed in any volume of voice

For those who knew her in her later years, the above representation was the image most solid in their minds. Mrs. Motley a model of the sort of middle-class woman that the race (Negro, Black, African-American, take your pick) first began producing in sizable numbers during the decade immediately following the Second World War. A cast comprised of many shades, these women were college educated and church going and married moms for the most part. Fluent in Standard English with impeccable cursive handwriting, the vast majority held down two jobs — a five-days-a-week job in a school, office, or hospital let's say, that paid a salary, and a non-paying, seven-days-a-week job of cooking, cleaning, and childrearing.

Yes, folks in Parkland, who were all Black and middle-class too (and don't you ever forget it: "Look at our well-kept houses," they'd say. "Look at our well-tended lawns."), thought they knew all there was to know when it came to Mrs. Motley. But we all have our unspoken lives, do we not? A set of confidential files stamped top secret that are locked in a combination safe that's stored in the deepest territories of our souls. And oh, what would people say if they only knew! If they had any idea what we're hiding!

Well Mrs. Motley was no different. She had her close-to-the-vest stuff too: her wedding for instance, which took place on 14 July 1946. The temperature was 89 degrees outside and much warmer inside the church, which like most houses of worship back then had no air conditioning; so many hand-held fans fluttering that Sunday afternoon, like a flurry of giant butterflies had swarmed into the room.

Sidebar: The church was Wesley-Allen A.M.E.— African Methodist Episcopal, where Mrs. Motley's paternal grandparents had been original members—her grandpa Brownlee one of the first deacons, her grandma Brownlee the first pianist. It was a two-story, not very big, redbrick building set a quarter block north of the Cal Sag channel, a manmade commercial waterway that in those days was only sixty feet wide. On Mrs. Motley's wedding day, the channel's brownish waters were viewable through the row of raised, translucent windows on the church's south wall. (Nine years later when the Metropolitan Sewage District widened the Cal Sag to 250 feet, the rocky banks would be just steps from that south wall.) At that time the channel also smelled from all the waste—industrial as well as domestic—that people dumped into it. That day there was a light southern breeze, which brought into the church a faintly foul smell, but did nothing to alleviate the discomforting heat and humidity.

As the Soon-to-be Mrs. Motley was escorted down the room's single, center aisle, wearing a silky white dress and full hat that her mother had made, arm-in-arm with her dark suited and beaming father (though balding and mustachioed, you could clearly see that day where his daughter had gotten her height, color, and facial features), She-the-Bride had tears welling in the lower rims of her brown eyes. Everyone watching, including her pale skin mother turned sideways in a front pew, and the dark suited groom — who was of a chestnut hue — standing in eager wait at the end of the red-carpeted aisle with the robed and heavily perspiring minister; all of them were sure that She-the-Bride was overcome with the joyous and high emotion of the moment as she stepped carefully forward to the tune of Mendelssohn's "Wedding March".

Yes, her emotion was high all right, but the feeling was not joyous. And no, it had nothing to do with her getting a case of last-minute cold feet. Earlier, as she was dressing for her big day, just she and her mother in the back bedroom of the large, wooden, four square house that Mr. Brownlee and his brothers had built with their own hands, her mother alluded to an incident that had occurred the year before.

On an equally warm and humid day, a Saturday afternoon, Mrs. Motley, who was Miss Brownlee back then, accompanied by her best Parkland friend Barbara Conley, had decided, on a whim, to go inside the Reno Lounge, a saloon on busy 127th Street. They'd walked or ridden past the saloon countless times since their childhood days, but had never entered because even though they were both twenty-two, back in those days it was considered bad form for a woman to enter a bar "unescorted".

Another side bar: Both women wore block sandals and tea dresses — Brownie's dress blue, Barb's white with red polka-dots; Brownie's dark brown hair a tad shy of shoulder-length, coiffed with a part to one side and the lower ends very curly; Barb sporting two large Victory Rolls that curled to the back of her neck.

While standing outside and gazing through the open doorway, it was Miss Brownlee (called Brownie by all her friends), who came up with the solution. "You can be my escort, Barb, and I'll be yours."

They sat side-by-side on red leather stools at the black wood bar. They both ordered whiskey and waters because that's what their fathers' drank. Neither was able to completely finish, much to the amusement of the bartender and the other patrons, who hooted and laughed after them as they stepped out the door.

By the time they had finished walking to their respective homes, someone (they never did find out who) had already phoned the news to their respective parents. Both parental pairs were appalled by what to them was, "fast woman" behavior. Fast being the word used then for a wild and sexually promiscuous woman.

Despite their ages, both young women received a stern scolding. Neither was falling down drunk, but their liquor inexperienced systems were tipsy, leaving both with a serious case of the sillies.

Barbara managed somehow to repress hers until alone in her bedroom. As for Brownie, (her mother detested the nickname), only seconds into her father's scolding, she started giggling there in the living room where the walls were covered with flower print wallpaper. With her short, full-bodied mother watching silently from in front of the fireplace, her father had stood in the middle of the room and shaken a forefinger at his daughter, his only child, and told her that she wasn't so old that he couldn't take a switch to her. That made Brownie laugh, and when he looked at her furiously, as furiously as he ever had, and ordered her to, "Go get me a switch!" like he had when she was a little girl (though only on a couple of occasions) Brownie started laughing so hard she had to clutch her stomach with one hand and clasp the other over her mouth in a failed effort to muffle her guffaws. Her father had demanded that she stop laughing, "Right now!" which of course only made her laugh more. When she saw the butterscotch tone of his anger-riddled face darken, she hurried out of the living room with a hand still over her mouth; she running not from fear of his wrath, but from fear that if she looked at that face of his one second longer, she'd fall down on the hardwood floor in a laughing fit.

From the living room she hurried through the hallway and then upstairs to her room where she closed the door and tossed herself face down on the brass frame bed that was covered with one of her mother's handmade quilts.

Her father didn't speak to her for the rest of the day (a tense supper-time it was at the dining room table that evening), despite her attempts to apologize. He refused to speak to her for much of the next day (more tension as the family walked to church). Her mother finally intervened late that afternoon and a peace treaty was worked out in the pink walled kitchen.

Though she never told anyone but Barbara, Mrs. Motley viewed the laughing at her father as the day when she felt, for the first time, that she was grown up. Which she supposed did not speak well of her, seeing as how it had hurt her father so, she not becoming aware of the severity of the wound until her mother informed her on the morning of the day she was to become Mrs.

Motley. It was just the two of them in Brownie's bedroom, her mom, whose nose and lips were full-bodied like her figure, was already dressed. Brownie was getting into her silky outfit, when her mom, without warning, came up behind her and said quietly into her ear: "Last summer, you made your father feel small when you laughed at him like that. I'm not talking about small in height. I'm talking about the other kind. The small you feel inside. A Colored man has to deal with a world that's always trying to make him feel small, that laughs at him, laughs at what he thinks is important. He doesn't need to get the same treatment from his own blood. So, promise me you'll never do to your husband what you did to mine."

Not surprisingly, that took a lot of steam out of Miss Brownlee's wedding day glee. Now she was the one feeling severely hurt. Hurt by her mother's words. Not because she did not see the truth in them, but because of the timing. Her mother had sat on that last searing line for what, a year? Her mother had stayed her hand and waited for the optimum moment, when her daughter's guard would be completely down, the tender spot of her daughter's wedding day joy completely exposed, allowing She-the-Mother-of-the-Bride to deliver a most telling of blows. And *that* is why, on her wedding day, in the heat and the faintly foul smell, when Miss Brownlee caught sight of her mother's smiling face at the other end of the aisle — Was it a sly smile? An "I gotcha" smile" — she felt her own breath catch and tears start. Afterwards, she had no memory of the ceremony. She knew she must have said her words on cue, and done the ring exchange okay, and kissed her spanking new husband with the right combination of happy-bride's enthusiasm and polite-lady restraint, because if she had messed up any of those things, her mother would for sure have told her in private afterwards; because that's how her mother operated, ever at the ready with a correction should an error be spoken or committed in her presence. But during the reception held on the second floor of the church, during the costume change in the reverend's office where she switched from wedding gown to dress clothes for the long drive to Michigan and a vacation resort that rented to Negroes, her mother had been nothing but complimentary. "You held up so much better than I did. You should have seen me the day I married your daddy. Nearly tripped over my own feet coming down the aisle."

Later, when she thought about it, and Mrs. Motley thought about the wedding day exchange with her mother any number of times over the years, she recognized that it was her mother's cheery disposition during the ceremony and afterwards that for some reason, was what really made her mom's softly spoken words hurt so much.

This was still true many years later, when Mrs. Motley herself was up there in years, which was long after she'd forgiven her mother, for what had happened on the wedding day, as well as a lot of other things.

Any number of people in Parkland would no doubt have been surprised to learn all that, just like they might have been surprised to learn that despite her long and strong ties to Wesley-Allen A.M.E., her most cherished memories of the church were not of big things like her wedding, or her parents' funerals, or in 2012, Wesley-Allen's 100th Anniversary.

What stuck in Mrs. Motley's mind were things such as...

She as a little girl, during Sunday Sermon, flanked high on either side by her parents while she kicked her legs back and forth beneath the pew.

As a teenager and new Wesley-Allen pianist, alone in the church on a rainy, Saturday afternoon, playing boogie-woogie on the piano.

Morning sunlight casting windowpane, silhouette shadow on the hardwood floor of the church's upstairs room.

At age six, sticking her head out a back window of the second floor with Barbara, the two of them pulling loose dandelion puffs into the air and talking about who they would marry when they grew up.

The gold watch chain looped across the vest of her grandpa's gray, three-piece suit that he only wore on Sundays.

Her joy at age five, when Wesley-Allen's minister said that as long as she followed God's rules she would be granted eternal life, which at the time she figured would be a snap since she was always good anyway.

The little kid thrill when while walking down a neighborhood street, she heard an adult woman say, "There goes Deacon Brownlee's grandbaby."

Sitting in the pew as an adult and forming the aisle flank for her son, and Mr. Motley forming the inside flank on the other side of the boy.

Reaching over to lay a gentle hand on her little boy's wrist to signal him to quit kicking his legs under the pew just as her mother had done so many times with her.

The damp-wood smell of the church's anteroom.

The hiss of church radiators during wintertime sermons.

Attending a wedding reception, at age seventeen, on the second floor of the church after Sunday Service, in December, and how the bride was angry because everyone there was talking about Pearl Harbor being bombed by the Japanese earlier that day and paying hardly any attention to her.

The plump sound a coin made when you dropped it flat on the plush felt circle inside the ringed gold of the collection plate.

Why these memories, mundane on the surface, stuck with her over the years Mrs. Motley could not have told you. All she knew was that they'd had taken root, and in their vividness, had grown mightily over the years.

They'd also brought her great joy whenever she felt a certain longing need that she could only satisfy by turning the memories over in her mind.

Now what surely would not have surprised anybody was that Mrs. Motley also had cherished remembrances of her husband; however, they might well have been shocked, especially when she was an old lady, by what those most cherished memories were.

The year before she graduated from teacher's college, which was 1945, on a sun bright autumn morning, while standing on the crowded station platform where she caught the commuter train into the city, she looked up from the folded newspaper she was reading to see a young man, in a gray suit and fedora, approaching her. He had to make his way in and around a few people, and when he reached her, he politely asked if she could tell him what time it was, as he had left his watch at home.

Although she thought he was more than a little handsome with his chestnut hue and thin mustache, she also thought it a bit odd of him to work his way over to her when there were plenty of people where'd he been originally standing to answer his question. Ever polite, she went ahead and checked her thin, leather strap wristwatch, a Christmas present from her father, and told the man the time. (Years and years later, she still remembered it had been 8:03.) The fellow doffed the fedora and thanked her with a smile that revealed a gap between his top front teeth, and when she saw the gap, the first thing that went through her mind was—what it might feel like to fit the tip of her tongue in that gap; the thought sending a charge through her that was as scary as it was surprising and delightful.

In her later years, long after her son had joined the Army, after her husband had died and her reputation as a reserved neighborhood widow was firmly established folks would have most definitely been surprised to know that on warm Sunday afternoons after church, Mrs. Motley would go to her bedroom, slip out of her shoes, stocking, and top clothes, carefully set them aside, and then stretch out on the high, large, four poster bed in her undergarments, which always included a slip.

There, she'd listen to the sounds from outside that made their way through the two shaded, street-side windows: an Amtrak train humming by on the railroad embankment one home east of her, children's voices, a radio playing, a car approaching or pulling away, a power mower at work, the chirps of birdies.

She'd gaze up at the white ceiling for a little while, never longer than a few minutes, then close her eyes and travel as if by magic back to the days when her son was a pre-teen, which was when he started the habit (that he carried all the way through high school) of leaving the house as soon as Sunday lunch was done. More often times than not, he headed to the nearby park, where along with other boys he played baseball in summer, touch football in fall, and basketball during the winter and early spring before the baseball started again.

It was her husband who first suggested they take advantage of their childfree afternoons to satisfy their private needs. At first Mrs. Motley had been reluctant to partake in such intimacies, coming so soon after Sunday Service and all, the reverend's sermon still warm in their ears as it were. But her husband had tricked her the first time by saying they would just lie down and nap. And for the first few Sunday afternoons that's all they did, but as time went by one thing lead to another, the temptation of her tongue tip wriggling against his tooth gap...

And oh, on how many summer Sunday afternoons, in the muted light of their bedroom, had they listened to the distant lawn mower, or the radio playing, or the train humming past, or the children's playful voices; she thrilled by the idea that none of the people connected to any of those sounds knew that while they were out there going about their business, on the second floor of the Motley's house, in the front bedroom, behind the swaying curtains, in the sweetest privacy, she and her husband were buck naked without so much as a top sheet over them because when the weather was warm, you wanted to feel that breeze ride across your damp body.

Because her doctor had told her that with her thin frame and pelvis, a second pregnancy would be risky; because the Sunday afternoon sessions started in the days before birth control pills; because she did not trust diaphragms (Barbara had by that time gotten pregnant while using one), Mrs. Motley and her husband pleasured each other in ways that made pregnancy an impossible result, she going to the bathroom immediately after to brush her teeth and bring her husband back a soaped washcloth to wash his hands. Her mode of giving pleasure (which she had never heard of until her husband introduced it to her) had shocked her at first. Over time she found enjoyment in it. Not for the act itself, but more so out of a pride of accomplishment when she heard him give voice to his obvious delight. As for his finger manipulations, his skillful touches brought her to equal levels of happiness.

Years later, as a widow living alone, when she would lie in the four poster bed on a summer Sunday afternoon, the bed where one winter morning she had awakened to find that her husband had died beside her during the night, Mrs. Motley would think of afternoons she had shared in that bed with her husband. She'd rub her bare feet together, tickling the ball of one foot with the toes of the other, her attempt at replicating the way he used to stroke her feet with his hands. Invariably, while enjoying this muscle memory, with her eyes still closed, she'd scold herself, tell herself she was too old for such foolishness, too old to be acting like some girl "fiddling with her equipment" (her mother's phrase), while locked in the bathroom, or under the covers late at night after you were sure your parents were sound asleep in the next bedroom. On those later year Sunday afternoons she'd tell herself to just take a nap, "and to stop acting simple," because doing wifely duty with your husband after church was one thing, engaging in solo indulgences after church was something else altogether. But the temptation was *so* tempting. Her solution? She compromised. She made a deal with herself. She promised she would only do the foot-to-foot rub for ten more minutes, which was more than enough time to reproduce an over-all comfy feeling that was reminiscent of the intense serenity she had experienced in the restful afterwards of those long past, "Sunday afternoon liaisons", as her husband had called them.

And sure enough, before even five minutes passed, she was asleep.

Even when she was in her early nineties, after she had buried a second husband, who she didn't marry until she was in her seventies (which is a whole other story), when she was in a retirement home, she still getting around okay with a cane, just not up to the daily tasks of cleaning and washing and cooking, or negotiating stairs; on those Sunday afternoons, in the privacy of her little room, after returning from Sunday Service at Wesley-Allen, the ride there and back courtesy of her granddaughter who'd taken over the duties when Mrs. Motley's son had died; even then, Mrs. Motley would draw the blinds and sit on her narrow bed, which wasn't nearly as comfortable as the four poster, but much easier to get in and out of. She'd take off her black soft-sole shoes and white socks (she wore only black soft soles and white socks now), so she could lie down and listen through the parted window to whatever sounds came her way from outside, the outside noises in competition with noises from the hallway — and she'd close her eyes, and gently rub her feet together — rub herself back to where she once used to be, to who she once used to be.

JOHN GUZLOWSKI

Chicago

We lived in a single room, slept
on the floor, went to the bathroom
outside like in the refugee camps,
but no one here spoke German.

At night we stared out the window
at the cars in the street. They struggled
in the snow where a green bus
sank into a white hill tall as a cow.

My father hugged me and said,
"In the spring the snow will melt
and turn to water," and I asked him
will the water be like the sea,
will a bus take us back to Buffalo
or will we sail on the hard gray waves
all the way back to Germany.

My mom said, "This is America,
and here's where we'll stay."

CARL SANDBURG

Chicago

Hog Butcher for the World,
Tool Maker, Stacker of Wheat,
Player with Railroads and the Nation's Freight Handler;
Stormy, husky, brawling,
City of the Big Shoulders:
They tell me you are wicked and I believe them, for I have
    seen your painted women under the gas lamps luring the
farm boys.
And they tell me you are crooked and I answer: Yes, it is true
    I have seen the gunman kill and go free to kill again.
And they tell me you are brutal and my reply is: On the faces
    of women and children I have seen the marks of wanton
    hunger.
And having answered so I turn once more to those who sneer
    at this my city, and I give them back the sneer and say to
    them:
Come and show me another city with lifted head singing
    so proud to be alive and coarse and strong and cunning.
Flinging magnetic curses amid the toil of piling job on job,
    here is a tall bold slugger set vivid against the little soft
    cities;
Fierce as a dog with tongue lapping for action, cunning as a
    savage pitted against the wilderness,
                    Bareheaded,
                    Shoveling,
                    Wrecking,
                    Planning,
                    Building, breaking, rebuilding,
Under the smoke, dust all over his mouth, laughing with
    white teeth,
Under the terrible burden of destiny laughing as a young man
    laughs,
Laughing even as an ignorant fighter laughs who has never
    lost a battle,
Bragging and laughing that under his wrist is the pulse, and
    under his ribs the heart of the people,

Laughing!
Laughing the stormy, husky, brawling laughter of Youth, half-naked, sweating, proud to be Hog Butcher, Tool Maker, Stacker of Wheat, Player with Railroads and Freight Handler to the Nation.

FRANK NORRIS

A Deal in Wheat

I. THE BEAR--WHEAT AT SIXTY-TWO

As Sam Lewiston backed the horse into the shafts of his backboard and began hitching the tugs to the whiffletree, his wife came out from the kitchen door of the house and drew near, and stood for some time at the horse's head, her arms folded and her apron rolled around them. For a long moment neither spoke. They had talked over the situation so long and so comprehensively the night before that there seemed to be nothing more to say.

The time was late in the summer, the place a ranch in southwestern Kansas, and Lewiston and his wife were two of a vast population of farmers, wheat growers, who at that moment were passing through a crisis--a crisis that at any moment might culminate in tragedy. Wheat was down to sixty-six.

At length Emma Lewiston spoke.

"Well," she hazarded, looking vaguely out across the ranch toward the horizon, leagues distant; "well, Sam, there's always that offer of brother Joe's. We can quit-- and go to Chicago--if the worst comes."

"And give up!" exclaimed Lewiston, running the lines through the turrets. "Leave the ranch! Give up! After all these years!"

His wife made no reply for the moment. Lewiston climbed into the buckboard and gathered up the lines. "Well, here goes for the last try, Emmie," he said. "Good-by, girl. Maybe things will look better in town to-day."

"Maybe," she said gravely. She kissed her husband good-by and stood for some time looking after the buckboard traveling toward the town in a moving pillar of dust.

"I don't know," she murmured at length; "I don't know just how we're going to make out."

When he reached town, Lewiston tied the horse to the iron railing in front of the Odd Fellows' Hall, the ground floor of which was occupied by the post-office, and went across the street and up the stairway of a building of brick and granite--quite the most pretentious structure of the town--and knocked at a door upon the first landing. The door was furnished with a pane of frosted glass, on which, in gold letters, was inscribed, "Bridges & Co., Grain Dealers."

Bridges himself, a middle-aged man who wore a velvet skull-cap and who was smoking a Pittsburg stogie, met the farmer at the counter and the two exchanged perfunctory greetings.

"Well," said Lewiston, tentatively, after awhile.

"Well, Lewiston," said the other, "I can't take that wheat of yours at any better than sixty-two."

"Sixty-two."

"It's the Chicago price that does it, Lewiston. Truslow is bearing the stuff for all he's worth. It's Truslow and the bear clique that stick the knife into us. The price broke again this morning. We've just got a wire."

"Good heavens," murmured Lewiston, looking vaguely from side to side. "That--that ruins me. I can't carry my grain any longer--what with storage charges and--and--Bridges, I don't see just how I'm going to make out. Sixty-two cents a bushel! Why, man, what with this and with that it's cost me nearly a dollar a bushel to raise that wheat, and now Truslow--"

He turned away abruptly with a quick gesture of infinite discouragement. He went down the stairs, and making his way to where his buckboard was hitched, got in, and, with eyes vacant, the reins slipping and sliding in his limp, half-open hands, drove slowly back to the ranch. His wife had seen him coming, and met him as he drew up before the barn.

"Well?" she demanded.

"Emmie," he said as he got out of the buckboard, laying his arm across her shoulder, "Emmie, I guess we'll take up with Joe's offer. We'll go to Chicago. We're cleaned out!"

II. THE BULL--WHEAT AT A DOLLAR-TEN

. . . and said Party of the Second Part further covenants and agrees to merchandise such wheat in foreign ports, it being understood and agreed between the Party of the First Part and the Party of the Second Part that the wheat hereinbefore mentioned is released and sold to the Party of the Second Part for export purposes only, and not for consumption or distribution within the boundaries of the United States of America or of Canada.

"Now, Mr. Gates, if you will sign for Mr. Truslow I guess that'll be all," remarked Hornung when he had finished reading.

Hornung affixed his signature to the two documents and passed them over to Gates, who signed for his principal and client, Truslow--or, as he had been called ever since he had gone into the fight against Hornung's corner--the Great Bear. Hornung's secretary was called in and witnessed the signatures, and Gates thrust the contract into his Gladstone bag and stood up, smoothing his hat.

"You will deliver the warehouse receipts for the grain," began Gates.

"I'll send a messenger to Truslow's office before noon," interrupted Hornung. "You can pay by certified check through the Illinois Trust people."

When the other had taken himself off, Hornung sat for some moments gazing abstractedly toward his office windows, thinking over the whole matter. He had just agreed to release to Truslow, at the rate of one dollar and ten cents per bushel, one hundred thousand out of the two million and odd bushels of wheat that he, Hornung, controlled, or actually owned. And for the moment he was wondering if, after all, he had done wisely in not goring the Great Bear to actual financial death. He had made him pay one hundred thousand dollars. Truslow was good for this amount. Would it not have been better to have put a prohibitive figure on the grain and forced the Bear into bankruptcy? True, Hornung would then be without his enemy's money, but Truslow would have been eliminated from the situation, and that--so Hornung told himself--was always a consummation most devoutly, strenuously and diligently to be striven for. Truslow once dead was dead, but the Bear was never more dangerous than when desperate.

"But so long as he can't get wheat," muttered Hornung at the end of his reflections, "he can't hurt me. And he can't get it. That I know."

For Hornung controlled the situation. So far back as the February of that year an "unknown bull" had been making his presence felt on the floor of the Board of Trade. By the middle of March the commercial reports of the daily press had begun to speak of "the powerful bull clique"; a few weeks later that legendary condition of affairs implied and epitomized in the magic words "Dollar Wheat" had been attained, and by the first of April, when the price had been boosted to one dollar and ten cents a bushel, Hornung had disclosed his hand, and in place of mere rumors, the definite and authoritative news that May wheat had been cornered in the Chicago pit went flashing around the world from Liverpool to Odessa and from Duluth to Buenos Ayres. It was--so the veteran operators were persuaded-- Truslow himself who had made Hornung's corner possible. The Great Bear had for once over-reached himself, and, believing himself all-powerful, had hammered the price just the fatal fraction too far down. Wheat had gone to sixty-two--for the time, and under the circumstances, an abnormal price.

When the reaction came it was tremendous. Hornung saw his chance, seized it, and in a few months had turned the tables, had cornered the product, and virtually driven the bear clique out of the pit.

On the same day that the delivery of the hundred thousand bushels was made to Truslow, Hornung met his broker at his lunch club.

"Well," said the latter, "I see you let go that line of stuff to Truslow."

Hornung nodded; but the broker added:

"Remember, I was against it from the very beginning. I know we've cleared up over a hundred thou'. I would have fifty times preferred to have lost twice that and smashed Truslow dead. Bet you what you like he makes us pay for it somehow."

"Huh!" grunted his principal. "How about insurance, and warehouse charges, and carrying expenses on that lot? Guess we'd have had to pay those, too, if we'd held on."

But the other put up his chin, unwilling to be persuaded. "I won't sleep easy," he declared, "till Truslow is busted."

III. THE PIT

Just as Going mounted the steps on the edge of the pit the great gong struck, a roar of a hundred voices developed with the swiftness of successive explosions, the rush of a hundred men surging downward to the centre of the pit filled the air with the stamp and grind of feet, a hundred hands in eager strenuous gestures tossed upward from out the brown of the crowd, the official reporter in his cage on the margin of the pit leaned far forward with straining ear to catch the opening bid, and another day of battle was begun. Since the sale of the hundred thousand bushels of wheat to Truslow the "Hornung crowd" had steadily shouldered the price higher until on this particular morning it stood at one dollar and a half. That was Hornung's price. No one else had any grain to sell. But not ten minutes after the opening, Going was surprised out of all countenance to hear shouted from the other side of the pit these words:

"Sell May at one-fifty."

Going was for the moment touching elbows with Kimbark on one side and with Merriam on the other, all three belonging to the "Hornung crowd." Their answering challenge of "Sold" was as the voice of one man. They did not pause to reflect upon the strangeness of the circumstance. (That was for afterward.) Their response to the offer was as unconscious, as reflex action and almost as rapid, and before the pit was well aware of what had happened the transaction of one thousand bushels was down upon Going's trading-card and fifteen hundred dollars had changed hands. But here was a marvel--the whole available supply of wheat cornered, Hornung master of the situation, invincible, unassailable; yet behold a man willing to sell, a Bear bold enough to raise his head.

"That was Kennedy, wasn't it, who made that offer?" asked Kimbark, as Going noted down the trade-- "Kennedy, that new man?"

"Yes; who do you suppose he's selling for; who's willing to go short at this stage of the game?"

"Maybe he ain't short."

"Short! Great heavens, man; where'd he get the stuff?"

"Blamed if I know. We can account for every handful of May. Steady! Oh, there he goes again."

"Sell a thousand May at one-fifty," vociferated the bear-broker, throwing out his hand, one finger raised to indicate the number of "contracts" offered. This time it was evident that he was attacking the Hornung crowd deliberately, for, ignoring the jam of traders that swept toward him, he looked across the pit to where Going and Kimbark were shouting "Sold! Sold!" and nodded his head.

A second time Going made memoranda of the trade, and either the Hornung holdings were increased by two thousand bushels of May wheat or the Hornung bank account swelled by at least three thousand dollars of some unknown short's money.

Of late--so sure was the bull crowd of its position--no one had even thought of glancing at the inspection sheet on the bulletin board. But now one of Going's messengers hurried up to him with the announcement that this sheet showed receipts at Chicago for that morning of twenty-five thousand bushels, and not credited to Hornung. Someone had got hold of a line of wheat overlooked by the "clique" and was dumping it upon them.

"Wire the Chief," said Going over his shoulder to Merriam. This one struggled out of the crowd, and on a telegraph blank scribbled:

"Strong bear movement--New man--Kennedy--Selling in lots of five contracts--Chicago receipts twenty-five thousand."

The message was dispatched, and in a few moments the answer came back, laconic, of military terseness:

"Support the market."

And Going obeyed, Merriam and Kimbark following, the new broker fairly throwing the wheat at them in thousand-bushel lots.

"Sell May at 'fifty; sell May; sell May." A moment's indecision, an instant's hesitation, the first faint suggestion of weakness, and the market would have broken under them. But for the better part of four hours they stood their ground, taking all that was offered, in constant communication with the Chief, and from time to time stimulated and steadied by his brief, unvarying command:

"Support the market."

At the close of the session they had bought in the twenty-five thousand bushels of May. Hornung's position was as stable as a rock, and the price closed even with the opening figure--one dollar and a half. But the morning's work was the talk of all La Salle Street. Who was back of the raid? What was the meaning of this unexpected selling? For weeks the pit trading had been merely nominal. Truslow, the Great Bear, from whom the most serious attack might have been expected, had gone to his country seat at Geneva Lake, in Wisconsin, declaring himself to be out of the market entirely. He went bass-fishing every day.

IV. THE BELT LINE

On a certain day toward the middle of the month, at a time when the mysterious Bear had unloaded some eighty thousand bushels upon Hornung, a conference was held in the library of Hornung's home. His broker attended it, and also a clean-faced, bright-eyed individual whose name of Cyrus Ryder might have been found upon the pay-roll of a rather well-known detective agency. For upward of half an hour after the conference began the detective spoke, the other two listening attentively, gravely.

"Then, last of all," concluded Ryder, "I made out I was a hobo, and began stealing rides on the Belt Line Railroad. Know the road? It just circles Chicago. Truslow owns it. Yes? Well, then I began to catch on. I noticed that cars of certain numbers--thirty-one nought thirty-four, thirty-two one ninety--well, the numbers don't matter, but anyhow, these cars were always switched onto the sidings by Mr. Truslow's main elevator D soon as they came in. The wheat was shunted in, and they were pulled out again. Well, I spotted one car and stole a ride on her. Say, look here, that car went right around the city on the Belt, and came back to D again, and the same wheat in her all the time. The grain was reinspected--it was raw, I tell you--and the warehouse receipts made out just as though the stuff had come in from Kansas or Iowa."

"The same wheat all the time!" interrupted Hornung.

"The same wheat--your wheat, that you sold to Truslow."

"Great snakes!" ejaculated Hornung's broker. "Truslow never took it abroad at all."

"Took it abroad! Say, he's just been running it around Chicago, like the supers in 'Shenandoah,' round an' round, so you'd think it was a new lot, an' selling it back to you again."

"No wonder we couldn't account for so much wheat." "Bought it from us at one-ten, and made us buy it back-- our own wheat--at one-fifty."

Hornung and his broker looked at each other in silence for a moment. Then all at once Hornung struck the arm of his chair with his fist and exploded in a roar of laughter. The broker stared for one bewildered moment, then followed his example.

"Sold! Sold!" shouted Hornung almost gleefully. "Upon my soul it's as good as a Gilbert and Sullivan show. And we--Oh, Lord! Billy, shake on it, and hats off to my distinguished friend, Truslow. He'll be President some day. Hey! What? Prosecute him? Not I."

"He's done us out of a neat hatful of dollars for all that," observed the broker, suddenly grave.

"Billy, it's worth the price."

"We've got to make it up somehow."

"Well, tell you what. We were going to boost the price to one seventy-five next week, and make that our settlement figure."

"Can't do it now. Can't afford it."

"No. Here; we'll let out a big link; we'll put wheat at two dollars, and let it go at that."

"Two it is, then," said the broker.

V. THE BREAD LINE

The street was very dark and absolutely deserted. It was a district on the "South Side," not far from the Chicago River, given up largely to wholesale stores, and after nightfall was empty of all life. The echoes slept but lightly hereabouts, and the slightest footfall, the faintest noise, woke them upon the instant and sent them clamoring up and down the length of the pavement between the iron shuttered fronts. The only light visible came from the side door of a certain "Vienna" bakery, where at one o'clock in the morning loaves of bread were given away to any who should ask. Every evening about nine o'clock the outcasts began to gather about the side door. The stragglers came in rapidly, and the line--the "bread line," as it was called--began to form. By midnight it was usually some hundred yards in length, stretching almost the entire length of the block.

Toward ten in the evening, his coat collar turned up against the fine drizzle that pervaded the air, his hands in his pockets, his elbows gripping his sides, Sam Lewiston came up and silently took his place at the end of the line.

Unable to conduct his farm upon a paying basis at the time when Truslow, the "Great Bear," had sent the price of grain down to sixty-two cents a bushel, Lewiston had turned over his entire property to his creditors, and, leaving Kansas for good, had abandoned farming, and had left his wife at her sister's boarding-house in Topeka with the understanding that she was to join him in Chicago so soon as he had found a steady job. Then he had come to Chicago and had turned workman. His brother Joe conducted a small hat factory on Archer Avenue, and for a time he found there a meager employment. But difficulties had occurred, times were bad, the hat factory was involved in debts, the repealing of a certain import duty on manufactured felt overcrowded the home market with cheap Belgian and French products, and in the end his brother had assigned and gone to Milwaukee.

Thrown out of work, Lewiston drifted aimlessly about Chicago, from pillar to post, working a little, earning here a dollar, there a dime, but always sinking,

sinking, till at last the ooze of the lowest bottom dragged at his feet and the rush of the great ebb went over him and engulfed him and shut him out from the light, and a park bench became his home and the "bread line" his chief makeshift of subsistence.

He stood now in the enfolding drizzle, sodden, stupefied with fatigue. Before and behind stretched the line. There was no talking. There was no sound. The street was empty. It was so still that the passing of a cable-car in the adjoining thoroughfare grated like prolonged rolling explosions, beginning and ending at immeasurable distances. The drizzle descended incessantly. After a long time midnight struck.

There was something ominous and gravely impressive in this interminable line of dark figures, close-pressed, soundless; a crowd, yet absolutely still; a close-packed, silent file, waiting, waiting in the vast deserted night-ridden street; waiting without a word, without a movement, there under the night and under the slow-moving mists of rain.

Few in the crowd were professional beggars. Most of them were workmen, long since out of work, forced into idleness by long-continued "hard times," by ill luck, by sickness. To them the "bread line" was a godsend. At least they could not starve. Between jobs here in the end was something to hold them up--a small platform, as it were, above the sweep of black water, where for a moment they might pause and take breath before the plunge.

The period of waiting on this night of rain seemed endless to those silent, hungry men; but at length there was a stir. The line moved. The side door opened. Ah, at last! They were going to hand out the bread.

But instead of the usual white-approved under-cook with his crowded hampers there now appeared in the doorway a new man--a young fellow who looked like a bookkeeper's assistant. He bore in his hand a placard, which he tacked to the outside of the door. Then he disappeared within the bakery, locking the door after him.

A shudder of poignant despair, an unformed, inarticulate sense of calamity, seemed to run from end to end of the line. What had happened? Those in the rear, unable to read the placard, surged forward, a sense of bitter disappointment clutching at their hearts.
The line broke up, disintegrated into a shapeless throng--a throng that crowded forward and collected in front of the shut door whereon the placard was affixed.
Lewiston, with the others, pushed forward. On the placard he read these words:

"Owing to the fact that the price of grain has been increased to two dollars a bushel, there will be no distribution of bread from this bakery until further notice."

Lewiston turned away, dumb, bewildered. Till morning he walked the streets, going on without purpose, without direction. But now at last his luck had turned. Overnight the wheel of his fortunes had creaked and swung upon its axis, and before noon he had found a job in the street-cleaning brigade. In the course of time he rose to be first shift-boss, then deputy inspector, then inspector, promoted to the dignity of driving in a red wagon with rubber tires and drawing a salary instead of mere wages. The wife was sent for and a new start made.

But Lewiston never forgot. Dimly he began to see the significance of things. Caught once in the cogs and wheels of a great and terrible engine, he had seen--none better--its workings. Of all the men who had vainly stood in the "bread line" on that rainy night in early summer, he, perhaps, had been the only one who had struggled up to the surface again. How many others had gone down in the great ebb? Grim question; he dared not think how many.

He had seen the two ends of a great wheat operation-- a battle between Bear and Bull. The stories (subsequently published in the city's press) of Truslow's countermove in selling Hornung his own wheat, supplied the unseen section. The farmer--he who raised the wheat--was ruined upon one hand; the working-man--he who consumed it--was ruined upon the other. But between the two, the great operators, who never saw the wheat they traded in, bought and sold the world's food, gambled in the nourishment of entire nations, practiced their tricks, their chicanery and oblique shifty "deals," were reconciled in their differences, and went on through their appointed way, jovial, contented, enthroned, and unassailable.

AMY NEWMAN

Bones and Doubt

I'm bones and doubt: starved, starved, starved.
But anyhow, going on and on.
The world released me and it felt like a kiss,
like a dead rabbit's eyes emptying out.

But anyhow, going on and on,
the days tumble out and the nights distill
like a dead rabbit's eyes emptying out.
What am I thinking of, excessive love?

The days tumble out and the nights distill
my pumping sweet-crisp, feverish heart,
what am I thinking of, excessive love?
The heart an apple? Not that again, not Eden.

My pumping sweet-crisp, feverish heart,
an old nostalgia peeled to flesh.
The heart an apple. Not that. Again, not Eden,
nothing doing. A hiss of its dead pelt,

an old nostalgia peeled to flesh,
spread out beneath the leaves, gristly, pearled.
Nothing doing. A hiss of its dead pelt
irregular and elegant as death, no more than that.

Spread out beneath the leaves: gristly, pearled,
twisting in worms, wearing me out, all this.
Irregular and elegant as death, no more than that;
none of your transcendence to write about.

Twisting in worms, wearing me out, all this.
The world released me and it felt like a kiss.
None of your transcendence to write about,
I'm bones and doubt: starved, starved, starved.

MIKE HOULIHAN

On The Eario

Danny O'Neill buttoned the little vest they made him wear as a bartender at the old Bismarck Hotel. He wasn't sure if his new gig was a promotion or punishment, but he liked it.

He was now working the afternoon and early evening shift in the tiny bar on the landing between the main dining room and the Walnut Room. The hotel called the bar "The Chalet" but to the politicians, wise guys, and gadflies who hung out there it was affectionately referred to as "the hidey ho."

The Hidey Ho was a little bar room with only six stools, two booths, a couple tables and a pay phone on the wall to call into the office. This was way before cell phones or blackberries: the eighties.

The most appealing aspect of the room was that hardly anybody knew where it was. Guys could get a nice package going at lunch and then segue back to the Hidey Ho to drink the rest of the day away. Need to check in with the office? Just pick up the pay phone.

Danny would stock the bar, light up a smoke, and stand with his butt against the cooler, as the first customer would stroll in around three. He got to know the half dozen regulars who dropped by almost every day and he was no threat to couples that met clandestinely for a few drinks before heading up to a room in the Bismarck. Yeah, Danny O'Neill was the host of Chicago's best sneak joint.

Reporters and PR flacks would laugh as they watched the ash on Danny's cigarette grow longer as he appeared to fall asleep between rounds for the boozers. To them Danny was just the skinny old white haired guy in the Bismarck vest who shuffled behind the bar refilling their glasses. But Danny O'Neill was on the eario.

Danny would smile through his white moustache and whistle a little tune as he shot the breeze with the guys from City Hall just down the street. He'd tell them of his days as a singer fronting big bands when he wore a tuxedo and crooned for the crowds at the Green Mill Lounge.

"I used to go by the name of 'Danny O'Neill."

The wise guys would ask him, "Well, what's your real name?"

"It's Danny O'Neill."

For some reason that cracked up the drunks as they knocked 'em back and turned back to their plotting and scheming for the spoils of the Chicago City Council. That's when Danny would go into his 'sleep' mode and appear to be nodding off, but he listened to every word they mumbled. They were fair tippers, not terrific. Danny had no illusions that they were anything more than friendly, not friends. To them he was invisible and sometimes Danny wished he was.

Behind his back they called him "Sleepy Danny". Danny knew that at least one of the regulars was a big shot politically. They didn't announce it to him but he could tell by the way the others would defer to the red faced fat guy. Danny had seen him mauling a young broad in the back booth of the Hidey Ho on a couple of afternoons, both of them drinking martinis. The guy would toss his credit card on the bar as they left and wink at him, "Cash me out Danny, it's nap time."

Danny had seen the guy's picture in the Sun-Times once. His name was Red Brophy and he was some kind of commissioner in Governor Jim Thompson's cabinet.

Late one afternoon Red was sitting in the booth with two of his cronies, all three of them goin' east on Ashland. Ordinarily they would be sitting at the bar watching "Jeopardy" with Danny as they banged their beers. But something was wrong and Danny could sense it. They whispered back and forth in the booth and sucked bourbon.

Red was very drunk and started to weep, his hands over his face. One of the guys put his hands on Red's shoulder and said, "What else could you do?"

The guy next to him said, "She really screwed things up."

Red regained his composure and lit up a smoke with his hand shaking. He said to the guys, "It had to be done." Just then his eyes happened to lock with Danny's and O'Neill felt the hair on the back of his neck stiffen and curl.

A week later Danny was home with the flu, reading the Trib when he recognized a photograph of the young woman Brophy had brought to The Hidey Ho. She was a former St. Patrick's Day Parade Queen named Paula Coleman and the headline read "Still No Witness to Deadly Hit and Run".

Danny looked at the picture from an old parade. The young blonde was 38, pregnant, and single, an employee of the State Revenue Dept. He felt nauseous as he went to the kitchen and poured himself a drink. Danny lit up a cigarette and picked up the phone to dial the Governor's Office.

The receptionist chirped, "Good afternoon, Governor Thompson's Office."

Uh…Commissioner Red Brophy, please.

"Who should I say is calling, sir?"

Tell…. tell him Danny O'Neill is on the line…'Sleepy' Danny O'Neill.

NADINE KENNEY JOHNSTONE

Loosen the Edges,
Flip Quickly

These days, my son wants things that don't make sense, like milk mixed with watermelon juice. Every night, he stands before the open refrigerator in his Thomas the Train pajamas. His feet are bare, his hair wet and curly from his bath. As he clutches two toy trains in his right hand, he uses his left to point at the cartons in the fridge. When I make his bottle, he says, "More red juice, Mama."

I try to explain curdling and tummy aches, but he still insists on this weird concoction. He wants what he wants, when he wants it. And when he doesn't get it, he becomes a flurry of flailing limbs. The parenting books describe this impulsiveness, how toddlers' brains are both babyish and mature, developing so quickly and yet so wrought with primal instincts.

My husband and I respond with structure and routine—day-care pick up at 4:30, then play time, then dinner at 6:30, bath at 7, bed at 8. At night, Jamie and I sit on the couch, discussing how to curb Geo's compulsions and avoid tantrums. Our only solution: more rules and routines.

This afternoon, I took Geo for a walk around Ravenswood—our Chicago neighborhood of children and dogs. I pushed his stroller down Damen, under the screeching brown line, then through the residential pockets of third-floor walk-ups like ours. After passing the library, we arrived at Welles Park. A little league team played on the corner diamond and it was pure summertime—boys in ballcaps, parents in folding chairs. Down the block, the splash-pad rained water on babies in ruffled bathing-suits, and the swings sailed giddy kids through the air. As we approached the playground, I noticed a distinct smell mixing with the dust from the baseball diamond—a light, doughy vanilla.

"What that, Mama?" Geo asked and leaned forward until his straps strained. He pointed at the Crepes in the Park stand—a little wooden lean-to no bigger than a fishing hut. Inside, two high school boys hovered over a circular hot plate.

Every time we'd walked past the stand in the spring, it'd been closed. Now, I had five dollars on me, but I knew I should be saying, *"No snacks, it's almost dinner."* With toddlers, everything non-routine has repercussions. Jamie and I have learned that when Geo gets too little sleep or too much sugar, he becomes the devil. You know that family at the grocery store with the kid tantruming on the floor for Coco Puffs? Yeah, that's been us.

In the crepe stand, the skinnier teen poured batter onto the hot plate and trained the other cook on the art of crepe-making.

"I want that," Geo said, trying to climb out of his stroller.

In that moment, I saw something of myself in my two-year-old, some instinct that desires the unknown and seeks it out, regardless of logic.

"Let's just see what they have," I said, which is exactly the same thing I'd said to myself when I was 24 and entering a crepe shop in Lincoln Park for the first time.

It was 2007. I had just moved to my tiny studio in the heart of Chicago's north side. Mom and Dad had deemed my decision to move impulsive, irrational.

There were logical questions: Why pay $600 for 400 square feet when I could continue living with them for free? There were safety concerns: What if I got robbed when walking home from the bus after night class? But, when I saw that Lincoln Park studio, I wasn't thinking in rational, responsible terms. I was simply thinking, *I want it. Now.* You see, even though the studio had a galley kitchen the size of a shoe box and walls with water damage from the bathtub flood in the upper unit, well, it also had a window facing East. The building in the next lot had just been torn down, so outside my window there was the shrine of St. Frances, then North Pond, and then Lake Michigan.

Lake freaking Michigan right outside my window.

Moving to that studio was a gut reaction to the news I'd just received that Jamie had been offered a new job, not in Chicago, as had been the plan, but in Massachusetts, and we'd have to continue our 800-mile-apart courtship. So, I had a couple options. I could do what I'd been doing—saving money and living with Mom and Dad while commuting to Columbia College from the burbs every day, or I could finish out my last year of school while living in the city.

I chose the latter.

I moved into my studio in August, on the cusp of my 24th birthday. As soon as I set up my day bed and my kitchen table in my little room, I did whatever I wanted whenever I wanted.

It wasn't premeditated. I just asked myself, *What do you really want to do right now?* And then, I tried to do just that.

What do I really want to do right now?

I want to sit in my pajamas and watch a marathon of Sex and the City *instead of going out to the bars with my friends.*

Sounds great.

What do I really want to do right now?

I want to spend my entire Saturday at Argo Tea, getting jittery on earl grey lattes and listening to Feist and writing.

Done

It was the most liberating thing, ever.

Try it. Right now.

What do you really want to do at this very moment? Do it.

But, usually, we have a big long list of obstacles that are stopping us. That was the wonderful thing about the year I was 24: not much was stopping me besides being broke. I didn't have to compromise with a sibling or a spouse. My life revolved around me and my desires.

Mostly what I wanted to do was walk around and explore the city. I took the red line home from Columbia, got off at Fullerton, walked east past the DePaul campus, peaked inside the windows of all the brownstones, then took a left on Clark and a right on St. James. Which was exactly what I was doing the September afternoon that I stopped in front of the Algerian creperie, Icosium Kafé.

I'd smelled that doughy vanilla scent during my previous walks home from the red line, but I was on a tight budget: $25 a week for spending-money, which included everything from caffeine to cab fare. I knew that I should be using my money on nourishing meals, but ever since I'd moved into my studio, I'd been perpetually hungry, which was how I always felt when I was in-love with life. I wanted to try everything.

The sign said "Crepe and Coffee Palace," and the interior did feel like a palace nook, with its draped fabrics and cupola cutouts. It was a Monday afternoon, and the few small tables were empty. When scanning the menu, my eyes automatically looked for grilled chicken, so trained were they to find the healthier option. But I saw a large jar of Nutella behind the counter, and I asked myself, *What do you really want to eat?* My mind chanted, *Chocolate, chocolate, chocolate, chocolate.* So I ordered a Nutella crepe with caramel and whipped cream. Just saying the words was a rush, like a drug deal, because I'd been programmed for over two decades to be *good.*

The wiry old chef poured batter onto a hot plate, and spread it with a mini rake. Then, in a matter of seconds, his thin spatula lifted the edges and flipped it. A couple moments later, he lifted it again and draped it over the spatula like a saddle. Then he smoothed the crepe out on the counter and smeared a glob of rich Nutella into the center. The Nutella instantly softened and spread. Then, he folded the crepe, drizzled zigzags of caramel, and used a sifter to sprinkle powdered sugar over it. Finally, he scooped a dollop of whip cream onto the top and sent it home with me in a Styrofoam box.

Throughout the two-block walk up Clark, the smells of hazelnut and caramel teased me, prevailing over bus exhaust and sewer fumes. When I got to my building, I bypassed my old-school elevator with its accordion pull-gate and climbed the stairs two at a time all the way up to the sixth floor.

It felt like the wildest thing I had ever done, like the bag swinging from my hand held sex-toys or swords. And, maybe, in a way, it *was* the wildest thing I had ever done, because when I entered my apartment, I locked the door and opened my curtains to reveal that beautiful lake, and I sat at my mini kitchen table that doubled as a desk, and I ate desert by myself for the very first time.

This wasn't the way I used to wolf down sleeves of my college roommates' Oreos, drunk in the dark. No, no, this was a ceremony. I could still hear September on the other side of my thin window — a mixture of taxi honks and lake wind — but, for the most part, it was sunny and very very still in my little studio. I sat at my table and cut the crepe into petite pieces. The Nutella oozed out and the powdered sugar dissolved into the pools of chocolate. The scent of crepe dough permeated my apartment. I forked a piece into my mouth and let it sit on my tongue until it melted over my taste buds. It was both light and dense at the same time. I chewed more slowly than I ever had, feeling so incredibly in love in that moment — with life, with Chicago.

In twenty minutes the crepe was gone, and in May I was gone too, driving to Massachusetts with a diploma in my hand, my possession in the trunk of my Cavalier.

Flash forward six years, and I was back in Illinois, with Jamie and a baby in tow. When we drove through Lincoln Park, I was shocked to find Icosium Kafé replaced by a modern salon and my lake view blocked by a tower of million-dollar condos.

What had brought me back home was that feeling, that hunger I just couldn't satisfy out East, that in-love feeling with life and with my city that I had experienced when I was 24.

Now at Welles Park, Geo was pointing at the crepes, saying, "I want that." The lanky high-schooler poured the batter and told the other cook, "So, you wait a couple of seconds for the batter to harden." He grabbed his spatula. "Then, what you do is, you loosen the edges, and you flip quickly."

Geo held the foil-wrapped plate the whole way home to our apartment, smelling it and grinning with the same anticipation I'd had while walking up Clark to my studio all those years ago. As I pushed Geo's stroller, I tried to put my finger on the feeling fueled by that light, doughy vanilla scent when I was 24.

It wasn't exactly that I had loved my city, though that was part of it. It was that I'd loved what the city had allowed me to do: to give in to my impulses.

It loosened my edges.
It flipped quickly.

QURAYSH ALI LANSANA

dead dead
heat on the southside

I.
last night, police cordoned the four square
blocks surrounding my house in pursuit of a thug
who unloaded on the shell of a gangsta
in the funeral parlor filled with formaldehyde
and lead. black folks scattered, staining
complicated streets. i settle in for summer:
the maze to the front door, running teens
from my stoop smelling of weed and tragedy
reminding my sons they are not sources
of admiration, praying that might change. not yet
june heat rises like the murder rate, gleam
and pop already midnight's bitter tune

II.
fifteen years ago, tyehimba jess
told me about a funeral home
with a drive through window.

you pull up, push a call button
through bulletproof glass a friendly
somber attendant takes your request.

moments later, casket open
your order appears for review.

at the time i thought it inhumane.
now i think about the abstraction
of friendship while counting bullets.

III.
is there an extra dead?
what is the term for dying again
when already? killing chi?

and what of the corpses that walk
my block in the anonymity
of black skin and white tees
filled with fluid?

GARY JOHNSON

Marquette Park
1976

While splashing hose water Saturday afternoon on
her staked tomatoes in the weedy patch alongside the
garage, Dolores Karkula, plump-looking in blue sweats,
long, gray, rag-wrapped hair up off her neck, was
surprised to find her husband, Hank, puttering at his
workbench inside the tiny garage.

Earlier that morning, before she stepped into the sun-
bright yard, they'd had words about Sunday's black civil
rights march that was set to come across the defacto
Western Avenue color line at 71st. Protesters were
marching from all-black Englewood into the Karkula's
all-white ethnic enclave of Chicago Lawn, popularly
known as Marquette Park—named for the Jesuit
explorer Father Jacques Marquette and his namesake:
the three hundred acre Chicago Park District site at
California, a half block from the Karkula's brick
bungalow. Now she noticed the side garage door ajar
and Hank's shadowy figure moving behind the dark
window glass.

When she poked her head inside and asked, "What

doin', Henry?" he answered without looking up in his flat rumbling Indiana drawl.

"Aw, nothin' much, Maw. Just makin' me a sign is all."

His rail-like frame looked somehow taller to her in his striped bib overalls and matching peaked engineer's cap he wore round the house in retirement. She watched him methodically dab a narrow brush into a can of black Rustoleum and smear the loaded bristles on a good-sized piece of cardboard he'd razor-bladed out of an empty refrigerator box left in the alley next to Rose Potempa's garbage cans.

With eczema-encrusted fingers steadying a flat carpenter's pencil whittled sharp with his penknife, he'd earlier sketched crudely in lead what he was now fleshing out with paint.

Curious, she stepped across the dirt-packed floor up to her husband, smelling first the sting of the paint, then a soapy whiff of Irish Spring on his clothes from his shower, and the strong, musty, male, sunbaked aromas of Hank's oil-dripping cream-colored '65 Impala, sweet lawn mower clippings, sneeze-y bagged fertilizers and rock salt—garage smells that always made her anxious, like she didn't belong in there, especially alone.

She saw black letters on brown cardboard, the half spelling of his first word: N-I-G-G. Graphite scribbles shiny like gun metal in the reflected window light spelled out the rest.

N I G G E R S
G O
H O M E!

142

"You gonna really stand on the curb with that thing tomorra?" she asked.

"Sure gonna," he said, dipping his brush while peeping over his wire bifocals at her startled, puffy face. She grimaced, showing ill-fitting dentures.

"Well, I just don't see the point is all," she said, retreating to the doorway.

Theirs was a running debate in their hushed two-person household on the controversy of the city granting two park parade permits—one for a neo-Nazis White Power rally, and the second for the black preacher-led march—and, more precisely, whether to acknowledge the civil rights protesters, who would pass directly in front of their house.

Quirky press interviews of the Nazi leader touting wacky supremacy theories and the delusional Englewood preacher calling for realtors to open house sales in the enclave to blacks had confounded Hank, the sensationalized coverage playing like bad sports reporting on the intellectual level of Spy vs. Spy.

As the day of protest approached, he'd noticed blue and white prowl cars and the occasional paddy wagon lumber past his house seemed on the half hour. And all this talk of black people moving into all-white Marquette Park and running whites out of town he thought bunk. Why, he rarely saw blacks in the neighborhood except maybe at the Sears at 62nd across Western, maybe bus transfers standing on corners along 63rd at Pulaski, Kedzie and Western. Still, he began his sign painting after he discovered his keyed-up, next-door neighbor, Bernie Kruger, spray-painting a message

on an old bed sheet hanging from his backyard
clothesline.

*   *   *   *   *

Snap-snap-snap was the sound Hank heard as he
walked out to his garage, and turned to see Bernie
hidden behind the sheet on the other side of the fence,
his darting shadow showing him furiously shaking a can
of paint.

"Mornin', Bernie," he called across his narrow yard.

Bernie stuck his smiling baldhead around the
hanging down sheet, its hem puddled in the grass
secured by bricks.

"Well, hello, Hank! Looks like you're gonna drive the
choo-choo train this mornin' in that getup."

"Up with the birds yourself, ain't ja?" With carved
face wrinkles squinched against the sun, Hank's fingers
jangled loose change in the deep, comfortable pockets of
his overalls.

"That's true. That's true, now," Bernie replied,
shaking the spray can. He stepped behind the sheet,
touching up with an audible *spisssss* the tall black letters
Hank could only see in reverse.

E T T E U Q R A M
S Y A T S
!!!E T I H W

"What's it say there, Bernie?"

"Marquette Stays White! What else!"

"And what's that for?"

144

Bernie poked out his frowning face, thrusting the can toward the street.

"Why, for that march that's comin' by here tomorra Sunday. Gonna hang it out front so they see it passin' by."

Hank stepped across his clipped lawn up closer to Bernie and grabbed hold of the cyclone fence that spanned his yard.

"Ain't juh worried you'll stir things up with that?" he said softer.

"No more than these other assclowns! Been readin' about it? Jeez. I don't know who's more nuts — wannabe Nazis with their arrogant Arian bullshit or the clueless blacks with their come-to-Jesus-gimme-a-house-with-no-down-payment-cause-I-deserve-it fantasies! And them marchers—who or why the hell they wanna be in the park at the *exact same time* as Nazis is beyond me, y'know? It's like mixin' turpentine and gasoline and strikin' a match! Like they all got shit for brains! I'm tellin' ya! Guess this is just me given 'em a lil shit myself, eh? Bernie Kruger style!"

"Y'spelled Marquette wrong," Hank said, pointing.

"What!" Bernie ducked behind the sheet, calling off letters, now just a voice and a dodging bald head shadow.

"'M-A-R-Q-and U.' Ah, Hank! You're jerkin' my chain!" He popped his head out. "You had me goin' there, buddy. I coulda screwed up. No doubt! Nuts as I am about all this." He shook the can, the bouncing metal bead inside clattering thickly around the liquid.

"Y'got your Pollacks, your Micks, your Dagos. Lugans here already thirty years and more. And what are you and Dolores again? Bohock? And me a Kraut, but mostly mutt. What's gonna happen if it all changes? Blacks move in and scare us whites away? C'mon. I mean it ain't happenin' here—yet. Hey, cop buddy of mine says blacks're movin' in big time around St. Rita high school—and there's been trouble."

"That a fact."

"Anyway, this is all I'm gonna do. Hang this thing up so they see it, right? I ain't goin' near that park or them Nazis. Nosireee! Couldn't pay me!" Bernie fixed his gaze on Hank. "So, you prepared to move, Hank? With that sweet sweet railroad pension of yours?"

"Me and Dolores aren't goin' nowheres. It ain't gonna happen—if it happens—for a long while yet." Hank kicked his loafer at white flowering clover buds spoiling his otherwise perfect lawn.

"Well, my advice? You just might wanna start packin' slowly—like wrappin' the crystal in newspaper in boxes in the garage—*somethin'*."

A breeze kicked up and the sheet bellied full on the line like a sail.

"Almost dry, I think," Bernie said. "Say, you should make you a custom sign—for the march. Like me. I've never ever done nothin' like this. Swear to God." As a testimonial, he raised his hand holding the can next to his face. "But I'm just so rattled by it all. Hadda do somethin'!"

*   *   *   *   *

Before his wife had had her bath and came outside to water and weed, Hank set about making his own sign, his pushy neighbor's bad seed idea drilled deep into his subconscious. Nearly trance-like, he slashed his box cutter at the enormous Kenmore packing crate in the alley, pried open his tiny paint can with a screwdriver, flicked his thumb over the dry bristles of his one inch wide brush.

The GO HOME message came quickly but looked lost in the middle of the cardboard, so he added NIGGERS, a common enough Indiana slur he'd never especially cared for or rarely, if ever, used himself. He had no idea why he was getting so deeply involved.

Sure, viscerally he understood how a guy like Bernie and the many Lugans living in and around Lithuanian Plaza—actually a dedicated stretch of 69th that dead-ended into the park at California, including such venerated Lithuanian-founded institutions as the Sisters of St. Casimir Motherhouse, Holy Cross Hospital, Nativity BVM Church, and Maria High School—would be up in arms at Nazis parading red, flapping swastika flags around their enclave. But Hank had nothing particular against black folk, many of whom he'd worked with in the B&O roundhouse.

So he couldn't quite say what had gotten into him, except to admit that he was secreting his sign making from Dolores, whom he knew would not approve. He didn't realize how affected he'd been by articles and letters to the editor in the *Southwest News Herald* and the *Chicago Tribune* that telegraphed longstanding white power structures in the city and the neighborhood were being seriously challenged by outsiders.

*   *   *   *   *

Once it dried, Hank carried his sign out of his garage, through the yard, back porch and kitchen, down the creaky wooden floorboards of the short dim hallway of his shotgun-style bungalow, past the varnished bedroom and bathroom doors on either side, through the bright dining room to the front room, where he propped it in the picture window facing the parked cars and tree-lined street. Then he sat down with a huff in his padded rocker next to the lamp table centered in the window.

"You can't put that there!" Dolores cried, bursting into the room, fussing hands boxing a flour sack towel, upset in her voice.

"Why not? My winda."

"Charles'll see it bringin' the mail! You'll insult him! That what you want? Such a nice nice man."

"Sure. He is. But he's smart enough to know that sign ain't for him. He'll know right off."

"What makes you think that for sure, Hank?"

"Cause I didn't make it with him in mind, that's what. He ain't never said nothin' about wantin' to move nowhere round here. Fact is, he never crossed my mind til you—"

"So, he's supposed to see that sign, read *your* mind, deliver our mail, and not think another thing of it?"

"Kinda. Yeah."

"And you can read *his* mind cause you just know he'd never ever move near the park if given the chance? That's why we moved here if you remember. The park."

As if finished with the conversation, his enflamed, dandruff-y eczema-covered hands gripping the armrests, Hank shoved his rocker up and back while turning his head to catch the sun flash of a passing car in the street.

Dolores stepped closer, towel flapped over her shoulder, a fist on either hip.

"Mister Henry Karkula, I think you're way off your rocker on this one. You mean you're gonna insult the man we give a nice Christmas card and tip to every year, and have such a nice rapport with — saying hello everyday and whatnot. You wanna jeopardize all that?"

"It won't! I tell you it won't, Maw!"

"Then, why make the nice black man feel funny?"

The sign stayed put in the window.

* * * * *

Around 12:30 Sunday afternoon, Hank Karkula was standing quietly in his striped bib overalls and engineer's cap out front of his house, his homemade sign held at his side, as whites swarmed the curbs, lawns and porches, jumping into the street past the line of cops standing guard to gape east down 71st for the black march to materialize. He had not yet realized what a bad influence Bernie was to convince him of doing something he would never on his own do. It was crazy. Kids, parents, grandparents, aunts and uncles and everybody in between lurking on the sidewalk, camped out on lawn chairs or the curb, racing up and back as if anticipating a parade. Many clutched homemade signs slashed with swastikas. A monstrous, gleaming-white police copter swooped overhead, its tremendous whirling blades clacking.

He was glad today was Sunday, a day Charles would not be delivering mail or a witness to all the commotion. He watched passing shirtless longhairs in bellbottom jeans and other rowdies in cutoffs cradling rocks in their T-shirts pulled out from their bellies like slings; greasers grouped on porches, drinking beer; gossiping mothers calling their kids. Who were all these people? Sure, he recognized neighbors. But the majority of the faces were strangers.

He wondered who would be in this march. Desperate, nappy-headed, glazed-eyed druggies who charged crazily at your car at stoplights in the black section, spraying water and squeegeeing your windshield uninvited, then begging a tip? Or would they be regular folk? Like the nice black man he'd just seen downstairs in the Sears basement tool department, where Hank liked to browse. Tools had been his life working as a machinist in the B&O railroad roundhouse. He loved tools. The heft and feel of them in his hands. The sharp metallic aroma they left on his fingers he brought to his nostrils to sniff.

The guy in front of him buying the Craftsman Allen wrench set was neatly dressed in dark blue uniform shirt and slacks. A factory worker, Hank figured, with glasses, five o'clock shadow, mustache and matching worker's cap. Just the way the guy's muscled hands snapped open his wallet with strong black fingers and clean pink nails told Hank he was a family man used to paying his bills on time and kicking in to the Sunday collection plate. A man of responsibility. Not some no account. He was polite enough and even talked white to the nice white cashier lady.

* * * * *

He could tell by the rambunctious crowd and the now harried cops that the civil rights march was fast approaching. Blue-shirted patrolmen snapped baby blue riot helmet chinstraps tight, pulled down facemasks, boldly waved billy clubs, barking at folks to get back on the curbs. Swastika banners hung from lampposts flapped in the breeze. Signs of all sorts were nailed to trees, being carried up and back, propped on the windshields of the few parked cars owners forgot to garage.

A chubby kid waddled by wearing a swastika T-shirt emblazoned with NIGGERS BEWARE! The stark message sent a chill through Hank, as had the tall black-lettered message he'd seen on the whitewashed wall of the neo-Nazi headquarters just up the street:

STOP
THE
NIGGERS

Now he felt funny about his sign. Was he finally seeing things through his wife's and mailman Charles's eyes?

"What a turnout, huh Hank?"

Hank turned. It was Bernie in a Hawaiian shirt, puffing a cigar. "Man, I got firecrackers I'm gonna blow off once they get here," he mumbled conspiratorially, patting his shirt pocket.

He showed Hank how he'd ingeniously clipped his MARQUETTE STAYS WHITE banner over his lawn with clothespins from street tree to lamppost. That way, he said, cops couldn't tell him to take it down. "It's my property! What the hell!" Hank didn't bother to remind Bernie the city owned the curbside parkway.

*   *   *   *   *

Hank was getting nervous. A palpable tension rolled down both sides of the street as raised voices blared from further east and spread through the crowd to where he and Bernie were standing.

"They're comin'! The niggers! They're here!" kids around him shouted to one another, pockets bulged with rocks.

So it's come down to this, Hank said to himself, not quite knowing what he meant.

He turned to the house and saw his wife's gray head and stern pale face in the front picture window. She half waved to him. She'd claimed she wanted no part of his folly. But he guessed curiosity had killed the cat. Unbeknownst to Hank, and to show off their pristine bungalow to the marchers, she'd swatted her trusty corn broom at candy wrappers and Styrofoam cups tossed in the front curb gutter by punks coming and going to the park. Moments later, when he looked back, Dolores was gone from the dark square of glass.

Seeing his wife haunted him and sunk him into a mood.

For thirty-two summers he'd sat on his porch steps or a webbed lawn chair in his shirtsleeves watering his lawn and flowers—or watched warm and snug from his picture-window easy chair fish-tailing, snow-covered cars spin their whining tires down the icy street, monitoring too his shoveled-out parking space, claimed by a two-by-four set across a pair of upended plastic pails. If he stretched his neck up the block he could see the park's huge elms bursting into the sky. For thirty-two years a nice quiet place where nobody bothered you. Back then, with his wife and him newly arrived to the big city from the neighboring hamlets of Garrett and Auburn, Indiana, Dolores's long dark girl-like hair framed her less rounded face.

Now with all these strangers crawling over his lawn and sidewalk and coming uninvited down the street, people he'd probably never ever again see in his lifetime, and knowing somewhere deep in the park parading neo-Nazis were holding a rally, he felt a stranger in his own yard. And he didn't like that feeling. And didn't know why he felt that way.

* * * * *

Whites, screaming their fool heads off, clamored to the curbs, shaking signs, banners, fists and fuck you fingers hammering the air. Hank, standing under Bernie's banner, watched a lone motorcycle cop putter down the middle of the street, then a walking helmeted white-shirted cop, a fancy braided club in hand, then, just ahead of the marchers, a young, white hippie couple hoisting a lead banner, which read RACISIM HURTS POOR AND WORKING PEOPLE — a message Hank couldn't wrap his head around. Following them were the blacks with signs up on wooden slats in colorful church-going clothes, some in dashikis and helmets, others with drums and whistles, encircled by a mess of strolling helmeted cops. A rag tag bunch for sure. And they were moaning the classic civil rights anthem, We Shall Overcome, while others clapped to a rousing chant.

> *Marquette Park!*
> *New Orleans!*
> *We'll get free of our enemies!*
>
> *Marquette Park!*
> *New Orleans!*
> *We'll get free of our enemies!*

Seeing black sweaty faces appear in ragged rows and hearing the screaming whites blot out the marchers singing, and then whites hurling a few rocks and bottles into the street, a queasy Hank froze in his tracks, and, heart fluttering, broke into a sweat.

The whites' clashing shouts fused into a mighty roar. "MAR-quette-PARK! MAR-quette-PARK! MAR-quette-PARK!"

"GO HOME! GO HOME! GO HOME!"

He couldn't hear Bernie yelling in his ear. Picket-shaking white marchers he saw walking alongside blacks made him feel funny. Why do they wanna get screamed at by their neighbors like this? To what godforsaken end?

A new chant he couldn't grasp burst from young white-helmeted marchers waving orange printed flags

reading, FIGHT FOR SOCIALISM/PROGRESSIVE
LABOR.

> *Power! Power! Power!*
> *To the Workers! Workers! Workers!*
> *Death! Death! Death!*
> *To the Nazis! Nazis! Nazis!*
>
> *Power! Power! Power!*
> *To the Workers! Workers! Workers!*
> *Death! Death! Death!*
> *To the Nazis! Nazis! Nazis!*

The raw deafening rage on all sides made the hairs on
Hank's neck stand up. And, fearing a riot, he cut his
wide, panicked eyes at the cops.

He was too old and too tired to fight. And who or
what do you fight when you decide to fight?

At the back of his mind he heard familiar Nazi
rhetoric going back a dozen years to kooky George
Lincoln Rockwell's troublemaker American Nazi Party
goons; remembered a decade previous the hysterics of
bursting bottles and rocks pelting Dr. Martin Luther
King Jr. and his nonviolent entourage marching in the
park for open housing; recalled hothead neighbors
continually grousing about the blacks, the A-rabs, the
Spics.

Why's it Chicagoans always gotta be pissin' and moanin'
bout somethin' or somebody?

Suddenly, he involuntarily focused his intense unease
on the black faces filtering past him. It was their fault

Hank's calm had been shattered, why he'd been upset and arguing with Dolores, why their kids and all the young people of the neighborhood moved out never to return from college—if they even went. Shuttered stores moving off 63rd to the Ford City Mall; jobs drying up— good jobs, like the padlocked South Works steel foundry; folks conditioned to sit in long gas rationing lines according to odd and even license plate numbers. At Sunday Mass the pastor warned the parish was shriveling on the vine; collections were down; why, they weren't even sure they'd be able to open the school come fall. *All this cuz of them.* All this very disconcerting to Hank.

Now, paralyzed with doubt and fear, standing lock-kneed, still as a statue, the crazed, screaming whites swirling around him, he faced his sign toward the street. It covered his entire chest down past his waist, and made his floating head with the engineer's cap shading his eyes appear disembodied.

"Well! Bout time!" Bernie cried in Hank's ear, over the roar.

Spying cops, a giggling Bernie peeled open his packet of firecrackers in a crispy red wrapper to show Hank a tangle of threadlike silver wicks braided into a single, thicker wick.

"Happy New Year!" he whooped, touching his cigar ash to its tip, which smoldered, then flashed, before pitching the smoking mess onto the patch of lawn folks had just cleared rushing the curbs. Spitting sparks, the firecrackers flashed white hot and banged something fierce in rapid succession, wispy geysers of shredded confetti-like paper springing up from the turf in a billowing puff to float and trail off dreamily like ghosts riding a breeze.

Thinking it gunfire, a startled churchwoman in a floppy sun hat slapped a black hand to her chest. Grinning, hysterical white boys and others whirled off the curb, cheering and cracking their hands together. Bernie yelped, bopping in place. A bitter-smelling gunpowder cloud crawled between Hank's legs.

He didn't understand none of it.

* * * * *

Though Hank had planned to let his painted sign do the talking, by the time the last of the chanting, drum-banging marchers had trailed past, furious, herding whites giving chase, he found himself perched on tippy toes with his clenched fist punched high above his head, yelling nonsense.

The sight of the now empty, rocky and glass-glittering street triggered a long ago childhood memory of Hank's. He remembered watching during a particularly exciting weekend visit to his Uncle Leo a solemn uniformed row of boys blowing big-belled brass Sousaphones, spiffy white shoes striding impressively in step away from him, the very last row of the very last marching band bringing up the rear of a bitterly cold and windy downtown State Street parade; and on its heels, gruff-looking guys from Streets and San in green coveralls with thick bristle push brooms and tremendously wide scoop shovels, scraping up the trailing piles of horse apples, their round-shouldered indifference reminding young Henry, in turn, of the sad painted clowns he'd just seen jumping in the shadows of the Ringling Bros. Barnum and Bailey circus at the Stockyard's International Amphitheater in Bridgeport.

"See! That wasn't so bad now! Was it, Hank?" a grinning Bernie crowed, tearing down his banner, wooden clothespins popping off branches to bounce on the lawn with a few twirling-down leaves. With a furious spinning motion of his hands, he rolled the flapping sheet into a tightening ball to toss in his alley can.

"I guess," Hank muttered, a little dazed. And emerging from the fog that was Bernie's spell, he shyly folded his cardboard sign, ashamed now that Dolores would confront him with painful silence once inside the quiet house—as if she'd caught him at something nasty, red handed.

Looking to the front window, dark now except for her gigantic cream puff-shaped lamp shade, he pictured his solitary wife in the dim interior, hunched over a sock she was darning at the kitchen Formica table, face crinkled in keen-eyed concentration, a cold cup of coffee next to her handy stenographer's notebook, in which she, with a steel-edged ruler, patiently replicated for herself verbatim each and every morning, a pencil-drawn grid of the day's *Chicago Tribune* crossword from the original puzzle she selflessly let Hank work in the newspaper.

DENNIS FOLEY

Pretty Please

"Please."

I am home on fall break sitting with my grandfather
in the basement room my parents set up for him just
over a year ago. He has all the essentials down here—a
32-inch TV, a gathering of his favorite black and white
movies, a gray couch that matches the color of his eyes, a
twin bed, a half-full bottle of Jim Beam, another full
bottle on a shelf.

My grandfather took a bad fall and broke his hip a
few months after I settled into my dorm during my
freshman year at DePaul University. My parents moved
him into the "dungeon," as he calls it, shortly after that.
Over this past year, Gramps has mended well enough to
get back on his feet. He takes occasional walks to his
favorite Taylor Street restaurants and bars, and to watch
the shrinking white-hairs, like him, play Bocce ball at a
nearby park.

"Please."

When I was younger, my grandfather would take me shore fishing at assorted tiny lagoons and lakes southwest of the city, places like Maple Lake, Turtlehead Lake, Tampier Lake, and Saganashkee Slough. Every now and again, for a change of pace, we'd venture into Southern Wisconsin where small lakes are as common as the age spots that currently map much of my grandfather's arms. Gramps would rent a row boat so I could taste what it was like to fish from the Badger state waters. We never caught much on any of our trips. But I didn't mind that at all. While fishing, my grandfather's lips moved. It was the only time this silent man really spoke. As we fished over the years, he'd talk about the Cubs, the Sox, the Bears, gentrifying neighborhoods, the Catholic church, girls, his mother, his father, my mother, my father, his "beloved Delores" who died when I was five, and he'd always wrap up by talking about "old man Daley," who, according to Gramps, "ran a city the way it should be run. Like a boss."

"Please."

My grandfather rattles the cubes in his empty glass and raises it to his lips, attempting to suck the last of the whiskey vapors from within.

"You still have more," I say, nodding at the bottle at his feet.

He snatches the bottle and fills his glass once again. This time he sets the bottle beside him on the couch.

"The bottle's half full," I say, trying to be cute.

"The bottle's never half full," he barks, his crinkled face aimed my way. "Never."

In the 1960s, long before I was born, my grandfather ran around with a flock of men with strange nicknames like Big Tuna and The Clown and Fish Eyes. He is my mother's father and my mother never spoke a word about any of my grandfather's doings with these men. My father also stayed silent. But when you're a kid growing up in Chicago and your neighbors and the parents of your classmates at school know or learn that your grandfather ran around with such men, you hear things. Whispers mostly. "That's all it is," my mother would say. "Whispers. Don't pay any attention to it." So I followed her advice. And after awhile, the words, the talk, the chatter, the whispers—they died out.

"Please."

One day, a few months before my grandfather broke his hip, he walked into my bedroom and found me, jeans at my ankles, masturbating as I stood over a towel watching porn on my laptop. Gramps was over for Sunday dinner and I was certain this wasn't the sort of pre-meal appetizer he'd envisioned. He didn't freeze or run shrieking from my room. Rather, Gramps closed the door and sat on the corner of my bed. I immediately pulled my boxers and jeans up and zipped before turning my laptop off.

"Don't worry none about that," he said with the wave of a hand. "That's natural. Nothin' to be ashamed of."

I didn't quite know what to say but I was happy as could be that Gramps didn't drag God, guilt and the burning fires of hell into the equation.

"There was a guy I knew a long time ago," Gramps said, "a guy I grew up with. He used to knock himself out three, four times a day." He laughed and patted the comforter on my bed. "Guy always had his sausage in his hands. Always."

I smiled.

"His parents owned a restaurant over on Racine. He told me he used to shoot his load into the Alfredo sauce his mom made in the restaurant kitchen." He looked at me and jabbed a finger my way. "That's why you should never get the white sauce when you order pasta."

I released another smile.

"He got whacked when he was 35. Right in the midst of doing the dirty deed." Gramps' face went blank and then he eyed me from head to toe. "He was a righty like you."

Again I smiled.

My grandfather wagged his head. "You shouldn't smile at stories like that," he said. "Guy's dead."

The following day I decided to do what I had never done, to do what I had always wanted to do but never did because sometimes it's better not knowing. I googled my grandfather's name. This is what I found:

- 11 arrests
- Suspected mob hit man
- Suspect in 8 murders
- Zero convictions

Three weeks after I conducted my research, my parents took me to my grandfather's apartment for dinner. We stationed ourselves on old wooden chairs with worn cushions in his front room watching the Cubs game on the TV while Gramps toiled in the kitchen. Spoons clanked against pans, the oven door was constantly opened and shut, and Frank Sinatra hummed a tune from the kitchen radio. When Gramps brought out a bowl of bow tie pasta with onions, tomatoes, green peppers, mushrooms and sausage in gravy to the dining room table, we joined him. The fresh bread and olive oil were already there.

"What?" I said as I examined the spread, "No white sauce?"

My parents bored holes into me with their angry eyes but those stares dissipated when my grandfather broke out into laughter.

"He knows," Gramps said as he sat at the table. He aimed his gray eyes my way. "He knows loads more than you think."

"Please."

The basement. This was the third occasion that my grandfather had made this request — twice over the summer before I left for my second year of college and then again today.

"Please."

The first time, Gramps sat me down and told me some of the stories of his past. The man who lived in silence was suddenly no longer silent. Maybe it was because another of his old friends had died that week or maybe it was because of the whiskey he now drank regularly. The details danced from his lips. Angelo Broggorio in the backseat of his 1963 Buick 225, bullet to the temple, blood staining Angelo's white suit. "That car was the color of butter. A real beauty. Made the same year JFK got shot"; Anthony Parrilli in a restaurant booth, bullet to the temple, his face falling into a bowl of spaghetti, his left pinky ring finger severed and brought back to Munson Tennerelli as a trophy; Geno Naughton—"the half-breed" as my grandfather called him—half Irish, half Italian, bullet to the temple, placed in the trunk of my grandfather's car, buried in a field near Twin Lakes, Wisconsin "so his family could never have the pleasure of burying him." Jimmy Riccardino, my grandfather's friend, bullet to the temple while masturbating. "He asked me if he could do one last thing before I croaked him," my grandfather told me. "I said, 'Sure.' Ya know, he was my friend, so I said, 'Sure.' I figured he might call his mother or his wife from the restaurant payphone or kneel down and say a prayer, but he didn't do none of those things. He unzipped his pants, spit into his hand and started workin' on his sausage. I let 'im jizz, and then I shot 'im." Gramps ran a hand across his balding head, patting the few wisps of white hair. "No others. Not like they say in the papers or on that internet thing."

What do you say to a man after he tells you such stories? What do you do when he starts to cry? What do you do when he puts a gun in your hands and says, 'Please'?

The second time there were no stories, just the passage of the gun and the same request. "Please." Again I pushed the gun back into his hands and wondered why he couldn't just put the barrel to his head himself and squeeze one last time.

"Please."

But this time, it is different. My grandfather sets the bottle of Jim Beam on the basement floor, painted a fresh coat of gray over the past summer. He swings his legs around me, lies down flat on the couch and straightens himself. He reaches down with one hand and pulls a pillow from the floor near the edge of the couch. "Pretty please," Gramps says and then places the pillow over his head. I marvel at how the couch borders my grandfather's body, a perfect fit for his smallish frame. His legs are perfectly straight, his hands now connected in front of his waist. And then I finally notice that Gramps is dressed in a suit and tie, with his favorite burgundy wingtips on his feet. All that is missing are the rosary beads and flowers. I lean in, set both hands on the pillow and press.

CARL RICHARDS

Hitler's Mustache

you just sat there
counting time
watching
the invasion of Europe
from your cozy seat
atop that lip, that
quivering
barking
hateful
lip.
Swastikas flying
storm troopers stomping
'Burn the Jews'
'Conquer the world'
'Mein Kampf'
it all came from that lip
and there you were
just centimeters away.
I would like you more
had you snuck out one night
as the madman
slept
and crept
down to his throat
and wrapped your furry arms
around his Adam's apple and squeezed.
That's how they'd do it in Chicago.
But you did nothing
other than sit
atop that lip
and sleep.

VACHEL LINDSAY

The Drunkards in the Street

The Drunkards in the street are calling one another,
Heeding not the night-wind, great of heart and gay —
Publicans and wantons —
Calling, laughing, calling,
While the Spirit bloweth Space and Time away.

Why should I feel the sobbing, the secrecy, the glory,
This comforter, this fitful wind divine?
I the cautious Pharisee, the scribe, the whited sepulcher-
I have no right to God, he is not mine.

Within their gutters, drunkards dream of Hell.
I say my prayers by my white bed to-night,
With the arms of God about me, with the angels singing,
singing until the grayness of my soul grows white.

THOMAS SANFILIP

Imperium

The night was desolate and humid as Sarita Rojas
stumbled home. Although she was only a few yards
from the back stairs of the three-flat walk up where she
lived, she lay on the ground too disoriented to know
exactly where she was. The taste in her mouth was
metallic and foul, the grit that stuck to her lips from the
cloud of dirt and dust she raised as she hit the pavement
found its way between her teeth, some cutting into her
full lips smeared with lipstick, leaving a line of small,
bleeding cracks across her full mouth. Except for a thin
wisp of black dirt that ran like a tiny dark streak along
its upper ridge, her upper lip was relatively untouched
by the impact.

   She could feel her right leg bleeding somewhere near
the knee, but the exuding warmth of blood strangely
comforted her, as if somehow a sign she was still one of
the living, though she had every desire at that moment
to be one of the dead, laying almost face down on the
pavement. Her high heels had fallen off her feet in
skewed angles to each foot, and her black mini dress had
lifted above her ample hips during the fall, exposing a

naked buttock. She had purposefully worn no underwear that evening, and although she had accepted money on occasion for sexual favors, this night she had not engaged any interested man.

She heard the phosphorescent buzz of a street light nearby, the distant wail of a police siren cutting the air, a rustle of bushes nearby, and the sudden screech of a cat as though being strangled by the neck, then silence, and the vague fear of being unable to move, catalyzing her at the same time to lift herself from the ground, to crawl if necessary to the stairs and the third-floor landing where she could at least knock, and her half-sister Lorena could hear and answer the door and drag her inside the kitchen without waking up the house. Is it possible I'm dead, she thought, lifting her head in a daze from the ground, looking one way, then another, then laying her head back down as if too tired to rise and ready to sleep. Fearful and acquiescent to her fate, she almost wanted to embrace death before daylight, before her mouth remained bloody and soiled forever.

She managed to make her way to the backstairs landing, staggering and stumbling up three flights of stairs in the near dark, finding her way up the seemingly endless spiral in a half-light that made her look more like an indistinct shape of matter than a human being. She grasped the door knob as if impossible to let go, knocking desperately in muffled, but constant raps on the door, until she realized in her disoriented thinking she had her key all along, tucked in a hidden pocket, sewn inside the waist band of her skirt. With her body jostling the rear door of the apartment, eventually Lorena woke, hurrying to let her in. Sarita, near collapsing, fell into a chair at the kitchen table almost the instant it swung open.

"*Que te pasa*?" hissed Lorena.

Sarita mumbled something indistinct, wiping a line of perspiration off her forehead that was dripping into her eyes, her head falling onto her arm on the table.

"I saw Rafael this evening," said Sarita softly, almost like a whisper, her head still buried in the crook of her arm.

"There's nothing in the middle of the night, except trouble -- go to bed!"

Lorena angrily turned off the kitchen light, disappeared into the shallow murkiness of the half-twilight of early morning light inching into the apartment. The room was left quiet and for a few seconds Sarita let her head rest against her arm in a kind of lost comfort that reminded her of her mother many years before who, in order to help her sleep as a little girl, would lay her arm under her head, until she drifted off. In the morning Sarita would invariably wake up feeling lost and abandoned.

She never woke when her mother slipped her arm out from under the pillow, and there was no way of knowing at what hour her mother quietly retreated to her own bed. But ever since then, Sarita slept with her left arm securely under head, and every morning there was always a twinge of emptiness when she woke. She felt that way then as she lifted her head from the table, feeling suddenly intense longing to see her two daughters. Struggling to her feet to shake the dull leadenness from her head that began to ache around the temples, she walked slowly to their room. A peaceful acquiescence fell over her as she quietly pushed the door open and saw two still forms -- Carmen, her oldest, and Celina, the younger -- sprawled on their beds asleep, a small fan whirling nearby, ruffling their hair in the humid dark. One of Celina's play chairs, with fat, red-petaled flowers painted on the back, stood in the middle of the room. Quietly picking up the chair, Sarita sat down near their beds to look at them as they slept.

Every so often she was comforted by moments like these, and so lamenting guiltily for abandoning them in the night to satisfy an oppressive hunger of body and soul, she eventually wandered back, incapable of mothering to their needs, too selfish and too insatiable. The thought was too frustrating to consider rationally, her mind numbed and fragmented from the long night's venture, weighing her down finally to utter mental and physical exhaustion. Like a somnolent, she lifted herself slowly from the chair and left the room, falling immediately to sleep on the sofa in the living room, not waking until almost noon, long after Carmen and Celina left for school.

The same feeling of guilt and abandonment ground into her stomach like the night before thinking of her mother, rolling on her side, burying her face in the sofa as if to hide from the forces tearing into her soul. It was not until she heard the sound of the refrigerator door shutting in the kitchen that she realized Lorena was still home.

Walking slowly into the kitchen, Sarita sat herself down opposite her half-sister, who at the moment was pouring cream from a small pale-pink carton into a steaming cup of coffee.

"You know," Lorena started slowly, "if it wasn't for me, your kids would never get a hot breakfast and this house would be a complete mess -- so what is this thing that drives you out in the middle of the night? You don't get enough from Roberto? Of course, he's married, and has to spend some time with his wife."

"I can have Roberto anytime."

"So what is it?"

"I saw Rafael last night," Sarita said enigmically, but falling short of words, she went quiet as if struck silent by the recollection.

"I've heard this a hundred times before, Sarita," said Lorena. "You better concentrate on your children. They need you more than any man. You remember Ruben, the father of your two girls, don't you? He left you after Carmen was born, then came back, only to leave you pregnant again? Now he's in jail serving time for how long -- who knows? But he's not coming back to you when he gets out!"

Sarita knew what Lorena said was true -- a part of her still clung to the man who seduced her at fourteen and had taken the best of her loyalty and devotion, and it was, in truth, only a fantasy. She would call his family almost obligatorily every Christmas to see if Ruben was at last home, and the answer was always an indifferent, "No," and it was probably true that Ruben was not there, and never was -- still in jail like Lorena said, probably forever -- so what difference did it make?

"You better stay home until the kids come from school," said Lorena. "I have to do some shopping."

The house went quiet when Lorena left, and Sarita sat for a moment, looking at the swaying tops of trees she saw from the rear window of their apartment. Sometimes two or three blackbirds circled above them as if miniature airplanes, crossing her range of vision like several dark spots against the sky, but this morning the sky was unusually bright, allowing her a clear view of Chicago's cityscape that rolled against a distant horizon.

In spite of the time she spent with Roberto the night before, her mind was relatively clear; but the fact that he was so thoroughly ruled by his sexual desires, that he could be manipulated and made to suffer so easily because of it at once bored and excited her. All the intellectuality in the world could not hide from her the fact that Roberto was simply weak, for she knew all there was to know about his petty hungers and desires; yet the fact that she could control his sexual responsiveness so thoroughly provided her with the feeling of self-empowerment she found no other way of attaining.

Roberto grabbed her around the waist with his right arm as they sat in the rear seat of his car, his left hand stroking the inside of her right thigh.

"What's the matter, Sarita?"

"You're such a fool," said Sarita with a condescending smile as she undid the belt buckle of his pants, all the while looking straight into his eyes with a paradoxical mixture of excitement and disdain; yet as the seconds went on, the urgency with which he wanted satisfaction only made her disdain him all the more, smiling devilishly before Roberto's startled eyes.

"*La bruja!*" he hissed.

Before the stark impression could fully register, Sarita lifted herself over Roberto, making it easier to pull her short skirt above her hips. The thought of making love face-to-face with Roberto revolted her; and although begging to see her face nearly every time they engaged in sex, invariably she turned away. She was capable of sending Roberto into almost immediate orgasm; and though no different than many times before, this time she was not so eager to give him any pleasure, but to satisfy her own. Eventually, nearly every one of his moves left him unfulfilled, enough so that as his tension continued building to some irresolvable pitch, she was the only one who could culminate it. He thrust harder and more uselessly toward satisfaction, pleasing her at the same time without any direct knowledge that he was completely in her control. When she climaxed, both fell back into the seat, neither touching each other, but breathing in short, alternate rhythms that soon made Sarita feel Roberto's presence again as cold and alien.

"Not even my wife is able to do it for me," he admitted. "Why is that, Sarita? And why is it you never let me see the pleasure on your face?"

"Go home!" Sarita said, suddenly tired of his questions, pulling her skirt down, lifting the handle on the door and quickly exiting the car.

"Come back, Sarita!" he yelled, and starting the engine, began following her as she made her way down Division Street, until it was nearly impossible to keep up with her and finally sped away.

Sarita's uncanny sense of smell took over as soon as she left the car, her nostrils like two glorious entranceways to the underworld, two subterranean caves from which exuded all her sensuality as a woman, taking in everything at a whiff. For her, they were her sole means of survival, her only true antennae by which all things just and unjust could be discerned and measured in the world, helping her distinguish between true evil and innocence.

"You're too beautiful," her father once said when she was young, growing up in Puerto Rico, keeping her inside, he said, to protect her purity from the world; but when she met Ruben at fourteen that purity was destroyed. When she saw her father to ask forgiveness with a full belly ready to give birth, he turned away angrily as he chopped stalks of plantain with a machete under the shade of a grass shack set up along the beach.

"I've come to see you," she said anxiously, but he simply looked at her with cold, dispassionate eyes.

"You've come for nothing," he said, without looking up from his work.

"You don't understand, Papa!"

"I understand enough!"

He turned back to his chopping with a vengeance, the machete dripping a clear, sticky sap that kept oozing from the pulpy stems of the banana vines he held firmly in hand. His forehead glistened with sweat that looked like tiny beads of silver stuck against his brow.

"I have no daughter!" he said.

For a second his eyes locked with hers, almost tearing with rage, her whole body yearning to submit to his punishment. Instinctively, he raised his machete in his right hand to ward her off as if a ghost ready to suck the very life-force out of him, that by mere proximity he would be poisoned by her presence. By then she had drawn back, crushed and fearful that he might bring the steel blade crashing into her skull, and she would be glad of it and peaceful in death, putting her out of her misery and exile. Instead, he merely waved her away toward the sea to which she almost solemnly, religiously turned, walking slowly into the breaking tide in a disoriented haze of tears that since then had never ended.

Somehow leaving Roberto freshened her mind. As she walked along the street, one man after another cast lascivious stares after her, their gaunt, haunted countenances glaring out of street shadows like reflected eyes of animals caught in the dark. She felt herself being metamorphosized as a woman by each one, and this, in turn, fanned her desires. She liked the way her mini-skirt wrapped around her hips, the way the night air hung like a blanket of soft velvet before her eyes as she turned west along Chicago Avenue toward Humboldt Park, where she hoped to meet Rafael to forget her insatiability, and escape the feelings of guilt at work below the surface of her psyche.

She thought of Carmen and Celina, and wondered if they were asleep and well, whether they were crying for her like she had for her own mother many years before as she approached the overpass leading into the park. It was then she saw Rafael standing like a stone guard below the lowest portion of the bridge that crossed over a paddling pond that lay like a blanket on the earth beyond view. Even in the half-dark she noticed his striking features -- jet-black hair, glistening and vibrant, grown long and tied in a ponytail, pulled straight back away from his face, revealing a perfect, almost classical countenance as if part of a centuries-old frieze of Mayan or Aztecan warriors, chins pointed to the sky, arms pulled back in strained poses, grasping spears against enemies crushed below their conquering hands. He looked at her coolly and unsmiling as though to assure her he had, in fact, seen as far as any man could see into her; that her played-out existential drama did not matter to him in the least, engendering neither his applause nor condemnation.

"So you've come for another lesson, huh?" he said, extending to her a toke of the reefer he was smoking.

Breathing heavily, without another word, taking the joint between his fingers, she inhaled without restraint, feeling the drag into her lungs.

Within seconds, her head reeled at its unusual potency. She suspected then something had been added, giving it more punch than expected. At the same time, she was trying to separate the aroma of marijuana filling her head from his familiar body fragrance, so strong this night, she could barely respond without feeling weak and vulnerable before his inscrutable gaze.

Once she was unable to pay off a drug debt which he immediately forced her to pay off in sex several times.

"No mercy for you!" he said leaning over her with a cold smile so he could see every anguished twist of her features.

She never understood how at that instant of absolute humiliation she could find him so perversely attractive, his half-open shirt showing a gracefully muscled chest and torso, the fragrant smell of his body drowning her senses, her eyes filling with tears as she swam in the beauty of his leering face inches away from hers. From then on, he became a kind of addiction, a necessary component needed to sustained her embattled psyche.

Sometimes she had given away sex, even for a place to sleep, when Lorena refused to let her in after a long night's foray. For a moment all her bizarre, self-destructive actions washed away in a stream of distorted realities, that she was overwhelmed with desire to touch him, that she might revel in the feeling of emptiness he brought over her with his body fragrance whenever she was with him, overawed by the unreachable essence of his being.

Even though she desired him to bring her down from her exalted height of sexual self-conceit to find the one weakness in her armor that would defuse her power, she longed more to be reduced in his eye in expiation for her sins. Each time he thrust, the fragrance of his being invaded her senses all the more, sometimes heavy, other times muted, encircling her as if irrepressible columns of smoke, and she consuming each tendril, one by one, fragrant and deep. Though she thought she could please him anytime, he was completely impervious to her.

As the minutes passed, Rafael was even more beyond reach, and the stronger he grew, the deeper her satisfaction. She realized then she was incapable of dominating his body as she had dominated Roberto's, and looking into his face, he looked into hers without a mark of pity, only a thin, enigmatic smile playing across his lips.

Afterwards, he held another reefer out to her. Sarita grabbed it quickly, and began running awkwardly along the wet embankment alongside the bridge, falling as she reached the top. Only then when she fell to the ground did the rich, moist aroma of the humid earth fill her nostrils, reminding her of death, listening to Rafael's mocking laughter reveling in her self-degradation.

"Come back, Sarita, anytime!" he kept shouting. "I'll make you feel good!" but she could hardly hear it with the earth so close to her heart.

BEAU O'REILLY

I Took The Santa Claus Job

I took the Santa Claus job because it was just around the corner from the place where I was staying. And I figured I could walk there, even though the only shoes I had were gym shoes and it was already December. I was twenty-seven, and it had never occurred to me — a job like that. The Santa place was in a small mall, where you could stand and look from one end to the other, the sort I had always avoided.

My wife hadn't left me yet but she was getting ready to. That whole year we had slept on opposite ends of the apartment and she had swapped religions again, hooking on with a black Southern Baptist Church, where she could play the piano and the organ and sometimes lead the choir. My wife isn't black. She's of Norwegian and Scottish descent. Small, wire-tight frame and bad skin — scaling, eczema. It's the skin that got her to turn to Jesus, she said. Christ had healed worse. But I don't think it was that. I think she just wanted something big and other that could take her and hold her. Our living room was piled high with all the books: the Book of Mormon, the Bhagavad-Gita, the Tao of Sex, all the Joseph Campbells. And for a while I kept up with all the reading, figuring that when the trouble came or, not likely now, things got better, we'd be in the same place.

The trouble has cost my wife. She's lost forty pounds (and she was always small), and I just couldn't get through the Book of Mormon. My wife loves the choir at the Baptist church. She thinks they sound great. And she's right. I've gone with her a few times, just to hear her play. Last week I went. It was a Sunday and, of course, everybody was dressed to the nines — stylish hats, broad brims piled high with flowers. Most of the choir were women, with these big, tremendous voices. My wife can't really sing. Now she could play anything. But those women's voices turn on a light inside her.

I stand at the back of the church with our son, Benny. He's just turned three, and to him the whole world is sound. Mostly because of his mother. She plays the big piano men — Duke Ellington, Monk, Brubeck, Bill Evans — every morning at the piano, filling the room, making the neighborhood jump. My wife has strong hands and, as they call it, an accomplished touch. At night she sings old folk songs — "She'll Be Comin' Round the Mountain When She Comes" – singing along in this loud, comical voice. Benny just thinks the choir is an extension of his mother, that that's where the choir comes from. Benny is relaxed, twirling in his space. His left leg is pumping and muscular. He's always favored his left leg, his right leg's slightly behind – dragging. I'm uncomfortable with the congregation. And they're interested in Benny: his sweetness, his curls. They want Benny to join the church.

My wife lets out this long, wailing note from the piano, her head thrown back. Now it sounds more like a scream than a melody to me, but she's caught up in the fervor of the hymn – flushed, bowed, beads of sweat on her forehead, saliva at the corners of her mouth, the eczema creeping up the side of her face, covering her ears, red. And for a minute I don't recognize her. Nervously I reach for my son 's hand and I'm uncomfortable about it. Benny twists away, trying to dance off into the crowd. But I don't let go. I stand there, clumsy, knowing something awful is about to happen.

This day my wife will give herself wholly to Jesus. The minister will baptize her on the altar—total immersion. The congregation will pull back the floorboards , exposing the pool under there filled with holy water. And my wife gets wrapped up in this huge choir robe; wrapped, dunked, and held under while the choir sings, "Shall We Gather At The River." I hold tight to Benny's hand. He just wants to go to his mother and the last thing I want is for him to be baptized here.

And then the trouble comes. His mother and I fight about this—freakishly, bitterly—accusing each other of things that can't be true, throwing things in each other's faces. I commit to hating Jesus, even though I don't really. And she commits to loving him all the more, and I'm sure she does. My wife starts going to church every day and I start drinking. Scotch. After a few weeks I'm asked to leave our home and I do. I return at times—visiting Benny, only the two of us, walking in the park.

I wonder, some nights, if things would have gotten this bad if we had stayed in Chicago. Things were already weird between my wife and me. She had threatened to leave several times, buying a bus ticket twice, for herself and Benny, but strangely, she slept through the alarm each time, the drama of breaking up with me giving way to— what? Inertia. Chicago might have been helping keep our family together at that point. It was rough, huge, solid and matter-of-fact enough to help me argue my wife into seeing my point of view, that the world was indeed a tough place, a place where you willed yourself through each day; but look around you, everything continues and in Chicago there's very little of God in sight, so we must be the ones who make everything happen. This idea, that will power makes the day play out , not something greater, held my wife's attention for only so long and by the third bus ticket, my wife found the strength to shake off Chicago's calloused common sense and leave, relocating two hours to the south, taking Benny with her. I followed soon after.

I still have my job at the Unitarian Church—the vegetarian lunch counter. I make and I serve the lunch. I work with women my own age. They're nice and we get along. It's been a good job. I'm able to bring Benny there. And it's very difficult to offend the Unitarians. But over the next couple of months I manage to do just that—sleeping with my co-workers, forgetting to lock the cashbox. There's an emergency board meeting, and all the ex-hippies on the board, they vote to expel me. And so that night, me and my co-workers, drunk and giggling, we decorate the front of the church with condoms filled with red speckles and wet blue Play-Doh. I take a placard and I write, "I'm being fucked by the Unitarian Christ" and I hang it up, but no one notices. And I'm tired from the months of drinking, but I don't really care. I take the Santa Claus job.

Now, the Santa place has a closet for the beard and the costume. There's nothing else there, just a chair. You're supposed to bring your own suspenders. And the Santa outfit already has the fat built into it, but my wrists stick out, and they're bony, and my face has gone all gaunt, and I can't do anything about it. So I practice the chuckle, making it warm, kind. I figure if I can get the chuckle down then I can avoid the "Ho Ho Ho." And the first few days are this blur of squirming children, alternately frightened and ecstatic. I chuckle, I pose, looking at the camera, raising an eyebrow, working the twinkle, the age. And in between poses I talk to the kids, keeping my voice low and calm. *They're so small*, I think. *No one should ever hurt them.* And on the third day an older boy comes. He's eleven or twelve, and he stands around the edge, watching before he takes his place in line. But he doesn't come too close. "You're not," he says, his eyes fixed on me. "You're not."

"I know," I tell him, "You're right."

And I remember how I held onto Santa Claus deep into my twenties, because I just wanted something big and warm that could take me and hold me. I ask the boy his name. He doesn't tell me. He runs off, kicking the earth. That night I walk over to my wife's place. It's cold. I need a scarf and a hat and I figure they must still be there hanging in the closet, but really I just want to see Benny and ask my wife when I can move back in.

There's no answer at the door but I still have the keys. I go in and there's no furniture, no curtains on the windows. I walk the apartment. No note. No roadmap to say where they've gone. I sit in the living room, my back against the wall, and I listen to the sounds of the empty apartment. Tomorrow I'll quit the Santa Claus job and if I'm lucky, I'll leave this town.

TONY SERRITELLA

Coming Home

The war ended in 1945. I was eight-years-old and it was about the same time I got my first paying job as a newsboy. I remember how excited the mood was about the war being over. Everyone wanted more than one newspaper, and everyone was in a terrific mood. There was hugging and kissing, even for me. The tips I got was more money than I thought even existed. I didn't quite understand what was going on, and I really didn't know what a war was. I used to walk by Victory Gardens, but what did this 'Victory' mean?

In my Chicago neighborhood, anyone that had a relative in the armed forces displayed stars in their windows, with the number depending on how many relatives were serving their country. The whole neighborhood over the age of eighteen seemed to have joined the army. They were all close friends and when one joined, all that could, followed. Just a bunch of neighborhood toughs thinking they could save the world.

There were stars in just about everyone's windows. Families were very proud that their sons were in the country's service. The sons were also proud of themselves, maybe for the first time in their lives. We had three stars in our windows: one each for my brother Billy and my two cousins, Danny and Joey. They enlisted when the war first started, and served three to five years. At my young age, I never did realize how long they were gone. My world was very small, and not too many people were a part of it. All three of them served valiantly in their combat duties. My brother didn't like to walk, so he joined the Air Force, where he was a co-pilot and bombardier. After his thirty some missions flying over Europe, he came home as a Captain with numerous medals. This was quite a feat for an enlisted man to rise to the rank of Captain. I asked him one time about his medals, which I heard about but had never seen.

"Yes, I have medals. I tried to make a bet at the race track with them, but they said no, so what good were they?"

My cousin, Danny, was an MP in charge of Japanese prisoners somewhere in the South Pacific. Joey was a 'combat engineer' in Europe. A combat engineer was the soldier who built the bridges so the troops were able to get where they were going. They were the real heroes.

And not once did I ever hear them brag about what they had done for their country. EVER. They were street kids, nineteen, twenty years old, and just did what they thought was their duty. The only time I ever did see my brother's medals was when we were cleaning his room after he died at the age of eighty three. Seeing the medals, I was sad that I could never show how proud I was of him. But not only him, my two cousins—Danny and Joey also. I never did show them the respect that they deserved.

I grew up looking at them as three happy-go-lucky guys that loved to gamble on the horses and play dice in the streets. Nothing ever seemed to bother them. They never took anything seriously, and this was the side of them that I got to know. They would brag more about picking a winning horse or football team than about all their heroic acts in the army.

In May of 1945, the whistles and horns were blasting in the neighborhood. People were screaming, dancing in the streets, and shouting "the war is over, the war is over, everyone is coming home!" The jubilation was something that I had never seen before, or heard again.

The celebration lasted for days. It was the first time, and probably the only time in my life, that I stayed up all night. Me, Jimmy, Johnny and all my friends. There was Waggins, a nickname he had because every time he hit the ball and ran to first base, it was like he was pulling a wagon. And Pinocchio, because he had a big nose and we told him that he had gotten it because he told so many lies. All my friends were up all night. It was such a festive time. These were memories that I would carry with me for the rest of my life. It was such a happy and proud time.

And never will I again judge someone by what I see. Just like an ocean of water. You can never tell how deep it is by just looking at it.

AMY NEWMAN

The Letting Go

Somehow I managed to let go of you.
You said you loved me deeply, but it was
not true, not true, not true, not true, not true.

The bees make sweets from pollens they accrue,
but I'm forgetting you with each day's buzz,
somehow. I managed to let go of you.

Regret's a dark, sweet nectar I fly through.
I'll make of it a honey labeled *Was*
Not True, Not True, Not True, Not True, Not True.

Let's inscribe those two words as a tattoo,
red inks indelible as my heart thaws.
Somehow I managed. To let go of you,

I'm pouring water on this crazy glue,
this airtight seal, whose lifetime guarantee's
not true. *Not true, not true, not true, not true!*

my heartbeat says. Oh fuck its point of view,
insistent muscle, pumping out red laws.
Somehow I managed to let go of you.
(Not true, not true, not true, not true, not true.)

PAT HICKEY

South Side Irish Soliloquy

Guy I Know - "Hey, Hickey! What's going on there,
son? I hear you been hitting the 8:30 Masses with the
roll-outs from Wrong's Tap. Last time I was in that
bucket o' blood was after Janey graduated from Queen
of Peace. I was in there with three guys from the
Assessor's Office and was still handcuffed to Mr. Booze.
Twenty years. I miss it not. Saw your cousin Willie at
that benefit for the Madden kid that got hit on his bike
over by Monroe Park. Tommy, the fourth grader at St.
John Fisher - he's okay but he has to wear that halo
gizmo for his neck. So, Willie's boy is in Paraguay, I
hear, with the Peace Corps, huh? Big Boy. Helluva
football player, too. I cannot understand why he did not
get a ride somewhere, but his brain works okay, I guess.
I'll bet the CIA or NSA is grooming the kid to be a
spook. True. That's why all the spooks doing the spy
stuff seem to come from the Peace Corps. Didn't know
the kid had Spanish.

Like I was saying, the last time I was in Wrong's Tap
was twenty-five, or thirty years ago. Remember Bubs
Murtaugh? Murtaugh with a U. He was a few years
older than me, when you and Willie and Terry played

Irish tunes in Sons of Reilly's Daughter at Boz's joint?
Bubs went to St. Laurence and played with Neusback.
He was from St. Denis Parish and lived near the tracks
on 83rd and Southwest Highway.

Anyways, Bubs got a full ride to St. Procopius—well
it was St. Procopius and it's now Benedictine out in
Lisle. He was an animal. Started boozing in 5th Grade
and sniffing Bell's Cleaning Fluid. His old man
threatened to send him back to the old country and
work the farm and shit. Bubs finally got tossed in his
senior year at Proco and his Dad got him on Streets and
San. Old Man Murtaugh was an off-the-boater from
County Mayo, who had some drag with Jackie Daley
and Kellam when he was alderman in the 18th.

Bubs was a good earner for the Ward so he got a
different job after a few years in Finley's office, just when
all that money grabbing crap hit the papers. Bubs had
only been on the job for a year or so and the G had eyes
on him and three others and it looked like he might get
tagged and have to sit for a few semesters up in Club
Fed, Wisconsin. We went out to forget his troubles one
night and Bubs marinated his brain, along with the rest
of us-- Mike Quinlan, Traffic Cosgrove, Bubs and me.

We're at Wrongs after closing Touch of Green and
Chez Joey and I got polio of the brain from the pitchers
and the Happy Cossack shooters, so Mike Quinlan takes
me home . . . I think. Quinlan goes back to Wrong's, after
slowing down to thirty and dumping me on the lawn,
and Bubs is blubbering to Traffic and Q-Dog, like a fat
girl not going to prom.

'I ain't took a dime! I woulda. . . but them tight, fixed
bastards that is . . . never gave me chance at the gelt and,

now, my old man is pissed at me for killing a good job and I told him, I DIDN'T DO NOTHING!' And on and on, I guess . . . like I said, I'm at home sleeping in my clothes on the basement couch and awaiting the for-sure execution from Marnie, when she sees the cut of me in the morning.

Now, Bubs has been named on TV by Ron Magers and his name was even mentioned in Royko and he's a public figure now. He's an innocent, drunk, lard-assed public figure. A giant sized victim and patsy all set for the shafting to come.

So Bubs, a practiced drunk driver, who has taken out more than several sections from *the fence that eats cars* on 111th over by Mount Olivet Cemetery, gets in his Pontiac and listens to the little wizard in his brain control tower telling him *it's a great idea* to go buy a dozen shrimp and off he goes to the Calumet Shrimp Shack on 95th and the River, by the bridge on the Harbor.

The Angel Fricken Gabriel takes the wheel for Bubs and drives the Ponty over east without killing anyone.

Bubs and the guardian angel drive the shrimp back, *somehow*, back to the neighborhood to dine *je suis ivre* behind the steering wheel and Bubs shoves the greasy catfish bait loaded with cocktail sauce into his hole and *tosses the sauce-heaped tails*!

Now, Bubs has gallons of Old Style, about a pint of vodka shooters and a good pound and change of sauce-soaked shrimps packed into him and he goes 'night-night' with his giant buffalo head on the driver's side window.

'OH SWEET MERCIFUL MOTHER! He's BLOWN

HIS BRAINS OUT!!!!!!!!!!!!!

There's about ten neighbors and his old man yanking Bubs out of the driver's seat.

It's daylight and Mrs. Higgins was walking her dog Chappie over to the tracks on Southwest Highway for his morning constitutional and sees Bubs' Giant Head covered in red! With Red smeared all over the driver's window, because Bubs never opened the window while tossing his shrimp tails! There's cocktail sauce all over the window and bits of shrimp! They all thought Bubs pulled the Dutch Act because of the spotlight on him!'

Never was charged. His Old Man beat the living shit out of him for the scare he tossed into him, and he had a hangover that would kill a large Polish girl. Bubs retired two years ago and still lives in his folks' house over in St. Bede's near Durkin Park.

Yeah, I stay out of Wrongs Tap. How's your kids, Hickey?"

DOMINIC A. PACYGA

Photographs and Memories

You see Paco what you don't understand is that we were all in Vietnam. The whole country was there. I know that's hard for you to understand being a real wounded vet and all, but it's true. You see it makes everything kind of blurry. I mean who is who and why? Pour me another scotch. I mean who are we, me and you, but the opposite sides of the same coin. Maybe even not so much the opposite sides. Nobody knows anyone else's story, really.

There is a black and white snapshot of my mother in front of Sacred Heart Church about 1950. I am sitting in a stroller and scowling while she smiles and pushes me down the sidewalk probably after a visit to my grandmother's flat in a tenement just on the next corner. The old brown brick combination church and school building stands behind us with vines growing up its side and a tall cast-iron fence surrounding it. Everything in that photo is gone except for me, and I am now sixty years old. Sacred Heart, the fence, the stroller, my mother, and even the sidewalk are gone. I always thought Sacred Heart would last forever. It was our neighborhood. The church stood as the center of our existence. Even the grass on the church grounds was precious, almost holy. That grass that Mr. Strzelski tended so devoutly is also gone. Mr. Strzelski, crazy as a loon and so guilty and devout, is long gone. So is the fat priest who smelled of stale cigarettes and scolded him for only receiving communion once a year. Some whispered that Strzelski was a Jansenist or some other such incomprehensible thing. Others said that he had committed some horrible sin in his youth. Maybe he killed someone! Everything on that block is gone. Even Strzelski's fascinating guilt has disappeared. So has his real or imagined sin. The landscape of my youth is as gone as if an A-bomb had landed in the middle of it and vaporized the buildings, people, all but the snapshot, the memory and me. The smell of my mother's perfume, the smell of honey-wax candles at morning Mass, my feelings of mystery as Father Karabasz, the only man I ever met who actually might have been a saint, said the ancient words of the Latin Mass, all are gone. The smell of waxed hallways, waxed by neighborhood women under the stern guidance of the Felician Sisters has vanished. So too is the smell of the stockyards that hovered over everything; "Roses are red, violets are blue. The stockyards stink and so do you." Sometimes when I am shaving I smell the Sunday morning smell of my father shaving. I look into the mirror and see him with lather all over his face and a cigarette in his mouth. The safety blade glides over his face and the voice of my mother tells my brother and me it is getting to be time for church.

Only ghosts remain, but even the ghosts are just memories and they will die with me as my children head for other places. My daughters will never know what I knew. Why should they? This is America and everyone moves on. The kids make fun of my memories like I made fun of the old ladies on Wolcott Street. Everybody in America makes fun. Fun is good. Guilt is bad. Everybody moves on. Even people from the Back of the Yards on Chicago's South Side move on. No one is guilty anymore. Now sometimes when I think of Strzelski's grass, I think that maybe guilt was not such a bad thing. Guilt makes good grass. You don't see grass like that anymore. That was a longtime ago. Now everyone criticizes good old Catholic guilt. From what I see we could all use a little guilt, but then maybe I'm just as crazy as old man Strzelski.

I can remember everything about that block. Every house, every smell, every family waits for me in some file on the hard drive of my brain. Burned in forever. Burned in just like the marks on Philip Wroblewski's chest where the fire from the helicopter, shot down somewhere out in the bush in Vietnam, touched him as he screamed running across a field filled with other young screaming men in the summer of 1969. A bullet hit him in the back as the jungle turned into an NVA shooting gallery. I sat in a bar on 47th Street as Phil fell wounded staining the jungle floor with his blood, the same Polish American blood that flowed through my veins. I sat in a bar not far from Sacred Heart Church and from Phil's mother's kitchen on Paulina Street. I sat gazing at a lava lamp, picking on the bowl of peanuts and glancing up at the White Sox game on the bar television. Wroblewski came home and sat next to me not long after that. I was the college boy. We were both drinking our way to some sort of place. The bar is gone too. It is now a taqueria. Old man Strzelski sat in a dark corner sipping a Pabst Blue Ribbon and just looked at us with that strange glare of the devoutly guilty. Mr. Papierz kept a picture of Nixon and Agnew above the bar, along with a photo of Franklin Roosevelt and one of Mayor Daley. There was a sign that said "Support Our Boys in Vietnam." Come to think of it that lava lamp was out of place. I think Papierz's daughter Cindy must have snuck it in one night. She left one day and never came back. Rumor had it she went out to California, but that might have been more fantasy than reality. Everyone wanted to run off to California. Most of us never got too far. Mr. Papierz always bought Phil the first beer of the day. He did until Phil told him to "take the fucking sign down." Phil and I thought that was hilarious. Everything was hilarious. A couple of shots of Jack and even Wroblewski's wounds were hilarious. He would lift up his shirt and laugh saying, "this one looks like Massachusetts. Here's fuckin Greece!" He'd laugh like hell. I'd break out laughing and we would have another shot of Jack.

Now old Phil had quite a story. He'd get tanked up and tell it at least once a month, "Well you see it was like this . . . our chopper pulled over the jungle and we came in at tree top. Green smoke rose up from the chopper down in the LZ and our damn bird came in. Two other birds hovered and started to land. Just then Charles comes out of everywhere--rockets, mortars... all hell broke loose, my man. Hottest little firefight you ever saw. The first chopper was already unloading and was caught with its pants down. We couldn't leave her there. Hot damn shit flying everywhere. The whole LZ started to go up. Suddenly the first chopper blew. I was on the ground. Our bird was hit next. My buddy, Forester, got it in the back of his head. The LT was cut down in front of me. The back-up choppers called in for support. I couldn't see any Dinks, but they saw us and that's all that counted. About thirty feet to the left of me some guys started firing at the tree line, but we had incoming from every direction. Mother of God I figured it was over. Another bird got hit and smashed into the ground like some fat ass pigeon hit with a BB. You know as I hit the ground and said some prayer I thought about you guys back here. For just a second I could see your faces, like you were standing there watching me. Goofy shit happens when you are about to buy your lunch. I got up and started to run. I felt something slap me in the back. Slapped me like when my Ma would hit me with the strap --- nothin much, just a dull smack across the back. It pushed me forward. My head went down. I tumbled like you would back in the schoolyard at Sacred Heart. There was something warm covering me. Suddenly the jungle started to go up as a shit load of fighter planes came in from the east. The whole fucking earth shook like a bowl of jelly. It certainly caught my attention. Then I passed out. Next thing I'm in a chopper. The medic says, 'you goin home you lucky sonofabitch, you goin back to the world.'"

Phil is gone. He died in a car crash sometime in the 1980s. By that time we had lost touch. I didn't go to the funeral. It was somewhere out in the burbs. Closed casket. Somebody told me.

In December 1968, right after Nixon got elected, I was on the verge of flunking out of college and being drafted. One cold December night I found myself in front of the Convent of the Poor Clares. Now the Poor Clares are a nice bunch of Catholic nuns who are cloistered --- that means they don't talk to the public generally except for one nun a month who answers the door. Frankly I don't even think they talk to each other, just to God --- or at least that is what I thought then and maybe still do, but anyway, the Poor Clares were kind of an institution on the South Side of Chicago. People would come to the convent and ask the good sisters to pray for this and that. There was an altar in the chapel that was covered with crutches, canes, and what not that people had left behind. My mother took us often to the cloister to say a prayer. It had a magical feel to it. The nuns would pray or chant behind a large grate that separated them from the public. I remember one hot day when I swear a statue of the Virgin blinked at me just to let me know she was listening.

So on that night just before Christmas I parked in front of the convent door and stood in the kind of slushy shit rain snow that makes Chicago famous. I rang the doorbell. Slowly a small nun pulled open the door. She was all of five foot tall. I must have looked quite the sight towering over her with my long hair and beard smelling of beer and Old Fitz and shaking from the cold damp December night. This was some strong little nun however ---- she was no post Vatican II wimp in a polyester pantsuit and cheap shoes. I am sure her name was Sister Mary Gelasius or Placidia or some real nun name like that. She would never introduce herself as Sister Eileen or Sister Judy or some other such modern I-am-just-like-you-only-different kind of way. This sister was the real deal in full nun outfit with a look that went through you to check out the mettle of your silly ass soul. When she saw me outside the door she just glared. The look was all business. I must have disturbed her prayers or dinner or whatever. The good sister said, "Yes, can I help you, my son?" I simply told her that I was flunking college and that I could already smell the jungle rot on my clothes. Sister smiled, snatched the five bucks out of my hand, told me that some people belonged in Vietnam and slammed the door. I got back in the dirt gold "64" and headed for the "Do Drop Inn" on 51st and Racine Avenue. You see I had kept the other five bucks I had in my pocket. No need to pay for too many prayers Paco, my man. Now don't knock the good sister or my brand of religion, I got off that damn probation list and made the dean's list every academic quarter from that point on. Now was it Vietnam or the Good Sister? Hell if I know.

There is another photo, an old color snapshot of me at about the age of twenty in my friend Pat Connelly's bedroom over on Peoria Street. I'm holding a bottle of whiskey and smiling. A map of Southeast Asia is on the wall behind my right shoulder. Jungle rot wore most of the picture away. Pat carried it with him in his wallet up in I Corps near the DMZ. We were and are the best of friends, at least in our minds. We don't, however, agree on much anymore. He is a Chicago cop. I teach at a local college. The college boy never left. Forty years later I'm still in the goddamn classroom. Pat and I agree on memories. Maybe that is the most important subject of all now that our neighborhood has disappeared into the damp jungle of urban America. Pat lives around the corner from me in our "new" neighborhood on the edge of the city. We hardly see each other and John Stasiak thinks that's pretty funny. He was the third partner in drinking our way across 63rd Street after Pat got wounded in February 1971. John's a Chicago detective. We went to De La Salle High School together, "Home of the fighting Meteors." He also lived on Peoria Street. "Photographs and memories" ----- it's an old song.

Another snapshot is of Carol Connelly, Pat's sister. She's sitting in an orange sweatshirt and blue jeans in her father's kitchen with a beer in her hand. CC's smiling with her Joan Baez hair hanging over her left shoulder. It was the night we began whatever it was we had. It was the first night Pat came home from Great Lakes Hospital after stepping on the booby trap up in I Corps. Phil Wroblewski had already moved on to other bars after old man Papierz told us to take our Fucking communist asses out of his Polka Time Bar. Wroblewski with his Purple Heart and Bronze Star thought that was incredibly hilarious and took a job at Central Steel on 51st Street. He did his drinking with work buddies after that and married Maggie Bishop at St. Gall's in April 1971. She had Little Chester in December. "Everybody has a hungry heart." Another song.

I found all three of these photos in a book, a novel I read a long time ago. It was stuck on a shelf in my office. There was also a newspaper clipping about another old friend, Wally Grabowski. Wally had a stupid, almost vicious smile. He combed his hair back in a "DA" a "duck's tale." He tried hard to be the toughest guy in Sacred Heart School. He wasn't. The nuns at Sacred Heart tried to pound the "attitude" out of him. Wally was always in trouble. He could hardly read and he drove Sister Stanislaus absolutely crazy. When he was seventeen he killed a cashier while holding up a grocery store on 51st Street over in Gage Park. Wally was always just plain nuts. It kept him out of Nam. Wonder where old Wally is today? Probably owns a 7 Eleven in California. Wouldn't that be a hoot? He probably smiles into the security camera every day. Life is like that. Sometimes it makes sense. Other times I think that God just has some ironic sense of humor that leaves you looking up at the night sky and laughing like some crazy old clown, or maybe crying like a Halsted Street drunk wishing his or her life away. Sister Stanislaus left the Felicians sometime in the mid-1960s. She went to live with her mother in Detroit, then she got pregnant and moved into a women's commune.

There was Johnny "Slow". That's what we called him. His real name was John Slowodowski. Slow had one kidney. He dropped out of Bogan Junior College in the fall of 1968. The draft board called him up. He told us he was gonna get some Cong. Bring home an ear. His girlfriend had a party. We all got shit-faced drunk. Brought him gifts. My mother cooked kielbasa. Only one that knew he was 4-F was Johnny himself. He knew he only had one kidney. Fucker got his 4-F and disappeared. The kielbasa was good. Mary's basement had party lights all around it and the phonograph played all night. Mostly Motown. What is it with working class white boys and Motown? I loved it, but never figured it out. I had a black friend, Jimmy Johnson, who always called me Bo or Bozo, when I worked with him at the shoe store on Halsted Street. He thought we were hilarious. "You know Bozo you should go listen to the Beach Boys or maybe those Chad and Jeremy whiney white boys, but leave the Temptations to me and my girl." Jimmy messed up the radio in the store so it only played WVON, the black station, Voice of the Negro. He would yell "We lissenin to VON, you Polaks!" Wally Wozak, another kid who worked in the store, hated it, but Jimmy was big and Wally was not. Jimmy drives a Coca-Cola truck now, married his girl, and lives in the suburbs. I see him sometimes in the Loop near my college. He has a good route. Raises his kids Catholic like his wife, Mary. Jimmy's mom, Mrs. Smith , a good Baptist, must be spinning in her grave. She was blind. Jimmy didn't go into the service. His dad died when Jimmy was a baby and he was his ma's sole support. Good people.

There was another black friend who worked with us, George Johnson. George took life pretty seriously. After awhile he went off to Vietnam. Jimmy told me George came back and found Jesus. Jimmy said "you know Bo you can't even talk to him without him sayin Jesus this and Jesus that and askin why am I letting my children follow some white man in a white dress in Rome! I told him I did it because the pope was your cousin anyway! "

Old photographs and songs bring back too many memories. Nothing is left. How did it all disappear? Oh well, time for the first of the day. I tell you Paco you pour the scotch and I'll tell you a war story, a real war story Paco. But not the war story you might think. Certainly not your war story or maybe even mine, but a war story nonetheless. Paco pour the scotch. Pour the first of the day!

BEN REITMAN

Conscription

Well, war has been declared. The love of Christ, the powers of the A.F. of L., and the influence of art, culture and literature were not able to keep America out of the business of wholesale slaughter any more than they did in Europe.

It is too late to worry about who or what caused the war. The war is here and our Government is spending billions of dollars like a drunken sailor in preparing men to kill quickly. It is no use to argue now about the right of justice of our joining the allies to crush Germany. Nor is there any use in trying to kid ourselves into thinking that this war isn't very serious and that it won't last very long. Most wars last from three to five years, and usually when a country has won a war, it goes in for other wars very soon. It is reasonable to believe that America for the next ten years will be in the fighting business. Just as soon as we have helped the Allies wipe Germany off the map, we are going to start in and clean up Mexico and teach Japan where she gets off at. And if the Russian revolutionists think they are going to run their country their own way, we may go over there and teach them to respect Government and our kind of Democracy. Besides, we have our eye on South America. While we have our big army and navy, we might as well annex some to the South American countries. Those Gringos down there don't know how to behave themselves, anyway. They are always fighting, and if they were under American protection, they would have more respect for religion and property and get along better. Yes, and besides—while we have our soldiers trained, we had better collect our war debts. We have loaned billions of dollars to Europe and maybe some of those countries who are fighting on borrowed money will get sore and won't want to pay us. Then we will have to fight to make them do it. I am afraid we are staring in on a long and brutal reign of militarism in America.

It looked for a while as though we were going to be safe, for even after war was declared, few men enlisted. The only ones who enlisted were those who were out of a job or disappointed in life and young boys who were full of life and wanted excitement and adventure. (They will get it.) Of course, if only the fool and the "no-account" would volunteer, we wouldn't object very much, but among those who volunteer are some of the finest young men in the land. If any of those boys will be alive in five years, they will be able to tell you of the horrors and uselessness of war.

But now we have conscription, and no one is safe. The thing itself is not new. All the countries in Europe have it. England passed its Conscription Law after the English workingmen refused to become professional murderers. At first, the bill also included Ireland, but the Irish were thoughtful men who knew history, and they said: "We haven't any more grievance against the German working men any more than we have against

the English toilers. *We refuse to be conscripted.*" And
when the government tried to force them to join the
army, *the Irish raised hell and began to kill the recruiting
officers.* Then the bill was amended to exclude the Irish.
And now everyone in Great Britain has to fight for the
king, excepting the fighting Irish and a GREAT HOST
OF CONSCIENTIOUS OBJECTORS.

Before the war broke out, there was much anti-
military propaganda carried on in England, and
thousands of people — Anarchists, Socialists, Quakers,
Trade Unionists and Christians — said, "Conscription or
no Conscription, we are not going to join the army."
And they made good. When the soldiers came around to
get these conscientious objectors, they said, "We refuse
to murder for our country or for anyone else." They were
arrested, and still they refused to put on the uniform.
They were beaten and clubbed and thrown into jail and
threatened with death, but they stood firm. Some of
them were carried in chains to the French front, but they
stood by humanity and refused to shoulder a musket. A
number of them were murdered by the English soldiers,
but nothing could make them desert their high ideals.
England tried everything to make soldiers out of these
brave men, but she failed and had to let them alone.

What happened in England was also repeated in
France, Germany, Russia and other countries.
Thousands of Italian Syndicalists and anti-militarists
refused to join the army. They were lined up against a
stone wall and murdered by their own countrymen with
machine guns. But this didn't frighten the rest of them,
and today in Italy conscientious objectors are respected
and excused from military service.

The Russians also refused to join the army by the thousands. The Dukhobors, the Tolstoian Anarchists, The Revolutionary Socialists absolutely refused to join the army. The government began to have these conscientious objectors shot, until they found some of their own faithful soldiers were killing their own officers instead of the conscientious objectors.

All along the French line there have been strikes of soldiers, but when soldiers have guns and bombs in their hands and are accustomed to killing, it takes more than mere promises to satisfy them. In certain sections of the French front, the soldiers refuse to stay in the trenches more than three weeks. They demand a furlough and go to Paris to have a good time. The French anti-militarists did not sell their souls to the War-Gods. They are demanding that their Allies, especially the English, take their places in the trenches. And this is one of the reasons the Allies are in such a hurry to get American soldiers on French soil. The French are getting tired of fighting for government, and are preparing to fight for themselves. It is not all together unlikely that when our American soldiers get to Europe, they will not be ordered to slay the Germans, but will be killing, French, English and Russian soldiers who refuse to fight for their "fatherland" any longer.

You may think that America is the freest county in the world. Yet we, the people, have no voice in making war. About three hundred men in the House of Representatives, one hundred and fifty in the Senate and one President have more power than we—the one hundred million American people. They can declare war—we cannot. They can stop wars; we cannot. No!—

Not unless we act like the Russians, and the soldiers lay down their weapons and refuse to fight. In Australia, which belongs to England, they tried to pass a Conscription Bill, but labor over there is organized and the working men said, "We won't stand for Conscription." You see, they didn't have a politician like Gompers who could deliver the entire organized labor movement to the authorities. Then the government said, "All right. We will have a referendum." They did. Although the government spent millions of dollars and all the newspapers howled and threatened, and the militarists promised everything, bluffed and cheated — Conscription was overwhelmingly defeated. As far as the making of wars and conscription is concerned, we are not a free country or democracy: we are just as much in the hands of "the King" as the Germans, the Italians or English are.

The English tried to get large numbers of Hindus and African Negroes to fight for them. They did succeed in getting a large number over to the French front, but the Hindus and African Negroes killed the English officers and then surrendered to the enemy. They felt that they would not be any worse off than their brothers are in their native countries. Now listen. Unless you get more information than the daily newspapers give you, you do not understand what is going on at the battle front. The only thing to remember about newspapers is that this present war is giving them a chance to raise their present price from one to two cents. War is not only a business of killing and destroying, but also the profession of lying, cheating and bluffing.

Conscription is now a law, but the law itself can't

change things. It has to have "force" behind it, and in a few months you may see all of those dear boys who volunteered into the army and navy, trained soldiers, armed to the teeth, compelling and punishing American citizens who refuse to be conscripted. We will need about fifty thousand soldiers to enforce conscription and we will need a great many more soldiers to keep the workers in line and prevent strikes. In war times, not only is your enemy dangerous, but every citizen who refuses to obey orders. He is regarded as an enemy to the country and may be brutally shot down. America fears Germany much less than she does men and women who refuse to murder for her benefit, and she will be a great deal kinder in her dealings with the external enemy than she may be with her conscientious objectors.

Since war is hell and we are all now in it, we might as well make the most of it. And if war means that we must maintain our honor and take revenge upon our enemy, let us stop and consider who our real enemies are.

Many of the men who join the army will suffer and be killed. It is estimated that a horse lasts sixteen days on the front and a soldier will last about eight weeks in the trenches. And so if we have to suffer and die, let us die for things we believe in, and suffer for a cause that will make the world a better place in which to live, and future wars impossible.

You have a life—you have brains and courage. Will you use them to make the greedy manufacturers richer and the government more powerful and tyrannical? Or will you use your life and intelligence to demonstrate that you believe in life and humanity and brotherhood, and that you are opposed to wars, poverty and injustice?

QURAYSH ALI LANSANA

reverse commute
for the burnout table

clock clanks inches
southward i wander

dance on tracks
like huck's jim

a woman nears
the tree-lined path

i clutch my bag
she sees bigger

in ill-fitting darkness
i see temporary harbor

bleached in halogen
at 8:17 the 8:13

train as suburbia
groves glens brooks

dusk in our hair
busy with nothing

city rushes to greet
wearing pungent night

MAHJABEEN SYED

How a Muslim Feels about 9/11

"Keep your head low." My mother said those words
to me shortly following September 11th. It left me baffled
and confused at the age of ten because I didn't
understand what my being Muslim had to do with an
attack that caused buildings to crumble like a heap of
brittle rocks over 700 miles away.

I accidently smashed my thumb in my mother's
Corolla door on the first anniversary of 9/11 as I was
getting out in front of my school. My mother's
traditional upbringing had taught me the value of
education so I went to school even though my thumb
had begun to turn the hues of a Turbo Rocket Popsicle.
Some distant and optimistic part of me reminded me
that I *was* dressed for the occasion. Red ribbons
complacently swayed with my pigtails, red shirt and
blue jeans making my white belt pop and it would be
such a shame to let all that effort go to waste.

Standing in the middle of a congested sixth-grade
classroom, right hand over my chest, feeling my
heartbeat race beneath my throbbing thumb, I distinctly

recall being aware of the eyes on me. Hushed and mental accusations that would eventually be verbalized hovered about in the form of impalpable waves that seared with hostility, the kind that 11 year olds were capable of anyway, and they were intentionally ignorant and unforgiving. An archaic recording of the national anthem roared louder than it should have and clumsily tumbled out of the intercom. A moment of silence followed and I detected the teacher taking a peek at me.

In that moment, an identity infected me, one that was given to me but was not my own. Was she looking at me for the same reason everyone else was or was my pain-filled whimpering not as silent as I thought? Was my patriotic outfit suddenly an act of over overcompensation? Would it be completely unbelievable if I said to them all that the two years I spent in India as a child I spent pining for America?

I was ten when I first heard the word terrorist. I was eleven when I was first called it. The kids who said it were mouthing something they had just heard on their television set, testing it out perhaps to see how it tasted. I often wonder if it tasted as bitter as it felt because that word would turn my three years in a grammar school where I was just one Indian among a majority of Hispanic students into years of uncertainty and camouflage. I would go on to join volleyball, cross-country and cheerleading to keep my mind and time filled and although you are supposed to be at the top of the popular hierarchy as a cheerleader, I would be picked on, not because I was particularly bad at any of the sports but because it was so easy. Because somewhere in the depths of the minds of other kids, they thought it was warranted. Three years of being bullied and only once did someone stick up for me and it meant so much to me that I still remember her name. Melisa Santiago, a very loud but very well-liked girl in my grade who was in the "in crowd" yelled at the top of her lungs, telling everyone to leave me alone one morning at volleyball practice when it seemed like everyone on the team was screaming at me for a serve that went sideways on the court. No one has stood up for me since then and this was 15 years ago.

I still remember that my school gave us small double-sided American flags that read, "We Shall Never Forget," to stick onto our windows to show our solidarity as a nation and as a people after 9/11. Later in the years, as the first anniversary of the attack passed and then the next, my mother would be harassed so much that her fears would lead her to get more American flags for us to display because just one flag wasn't enough to convince the public that not all Muslims were terrorists, because just one flag wasn't enough patriotism for a Muslim family — even if they had lived here practically all of their lives.

When I talk about Americans, I say "we" because I am American born and consider myself to be American. But somewhere between that time of mourning and chaos, "we" became an "other."

15 years have passed and I look around at Chicago and wonder how much 9/11 has shaped it. Because I already know how it shaped the country as a whole. When I read articles about the Muslim Brotherhood or about an Indian woman being crowned Miss America or any article that has to do with the Middle East, Islamists

or Muslims, I find my fingers scrolling down to the comments. There are usually thousands of them and the majority are heinous. People lump everyone who is Indian, Pakistani, Middle Eastern, Arab, whether they are Hindu, Christian or Buddhist into one box and throw a label on them as "terrorists." They propose genocide, to exterminate a massive population of people because of an attack that the majority of "us" had nothing to do with. With what the media chooses to cover and how they choose to depict anyone who is Indian or of the Islamic faith, "we" never stand a chance.

I don't believe that you can make the world stronger by oppression.

A sweet chill fills the air in September and the nation comes together and curls in upon itself like a Venus flytrap to remember and to mourn and subconsciously to reaffirm their distaste for "my kind." I become more aware of being the only Indian person at a coffee shop or on the bus or at the supermarket or at the DMV or…

And I wish that I could grab my loved ones and keep them with me in one safe place so I won't have to be afraid that someone will treat them unkindly because of their anger and it's so sad because this isn't the America that I remember wanting to come home to.

Every year I wonder, Ground Zero gets to be rebuilt. But will we?

IVAN JENSEN

Midwest Juliet

You fade into
sentimental focus
the wind
like a director
tousles your hair
you are on my
horizon
and just when
I think I understand
that telling look,
you turn into
a Rafael profile
and there we are
under
the migration
of the wings
of our affair
which just had to go south
like birds
the shape of flying lips
and the touch
of our ring-less
fingers
but I now walk alone
on the sands
of Central Time
like a hobo
catching another
vagabond train of
thought
my hands

remembering
the now dry harvest
texture of our love
knowing we
still breathe together
as one in the jagged
edges of the jaded
Windy City
we were the late
great lovers
on the lake
until you
took what I said
to the melancholy
midtown of your heart
now you are
just Autumn's
ingenue
who maybe
thinks of me
as I picture you,
my time filtered
Instagram,
the all American
girl next door
who got away
but I will
always
picture you perfect
before you
hid behind
your tangled
thoughts
leaving me
with those
'ole Chicago blues

CONTRIBUTORS

STUART DYBEK- is the author of five books of fiction—*Paper Lantern, Ecstatic Cahoots, I Sailed With Magellan, The Coast of Chicago,* and *Childhood and Other Neighborhoods,* and two collections of poems — *Streets in Their Own Ink* and *Brass Knuckles. The Coast of Chicago* was a One Book One Chicago selection. His work has appeared in *Harpers, The New Yorker, Poetry, The Atlantic, Tin House* and numerous other magazines and journals, and been widely anthologized, including work in both *Best American Poetry* and *Best American Fiction.* Among Dybek's awards are a PEN/Malamud Prize "for distinguished achievement in the short story," a Whiting Writers Award, Lannan Award, several O.Henry Prizes, and fellowships from the NEA and the Guggenheim Foundation. In 2007 Dybek was awarded a John D. and Catherine T. MacArthur Foundation Fellowship. He is currently the Distinguished Writer in Residence at Northwestern University. "Field Trips" appeared in *Harper's Magazine* and "Clothespins" in *Brass Knuckles.*

RICK KOGAN - Born and raised and still living in Chicago, Rick Kogan has worked for the *Chicago Daily News, Chicago Sun-Times* and the *Chicago Tribune,* where he is currently a senior writer and columnist. Named Chicago's Best Reporter in 1999 and inducted into the Chicago Journalism Hall of Fame in 2003, he is currently host of "After Hours with Rick Kogan" on WGN radio. He is the author of a dozen books, including *Everybody Pays: Two Men, One Murder and the Price of Truth* (with Maurice Possley); *America's Mom: The Life, Lessons and Legacy of Ann Landers; A Chicago Tavern, the history of the Billy Goat;* and *Sidewalks I* and *Sidewalks II,* collections of his columns and the work of photographer Charles Osgood.

JOHN GUZLOWSKI – John's writing appears in Garrison Keillor's *Writer's Almanac, Ontario Review, North American Review, Salon.Com, Rattle, Atticus Review,* and many other print and online journals here and abroad. His first novel *Suitcase Charlie,* a mystery set among Holocaust survivors in Chicago, is available from Amazon. His poems and personal essays about his parents' experiences as slave laborers in Nazi Germany and refugees making a life for themselves in Chicago appear in his memoir in prose and poetry, *Echoes of Tattered Tongues (Aquila Polonica Press).* Of Guzlowski's writing, Nobel Laureate Czeslaw Milosz said, "He has an astonishing ability for grasping reality." "Looking for Work in America" and "Chicago" first appeared in *Echoes of Tattered Tongues: Memory Unfolded* (Aquilla Polinica Press).

PATRICIA ANN McNAIR – A Midwesterner for 98 percent of her life, McNair has managed a gas station, sold pots and pans door to door, tended bar and breaded mushrooms, worked on the trading floor of the Chicago Mercantile Exchange and taught aerobics. Today she is an Associate Professor in the Department of Creative Writing of Columbia College Chicago, where she directs the undergraduate fiction program. McNair's short story collection, *The Temple of Air,* was awarded Book of the Year by the Chicago Writers Association, Southern Illinois University's Devil's Kitchen Reading Award, and a finalist award by the Society of Midland Authors. Her fiction and creative nonfiction have been published widely and received a number of honors including Pushcart Prize nominations, four Illinois Arts Council Awards, and the Solstice Short Story Award. She is currently at work on a novel, *Climbing the House of God Hill,* and a collection of essays, *And These Are the*

Good Times. Her story *Back to the Water's Edge* first appeared in the *Great Lakes Review.*

JOE MENO – is a fiction writer and playwright who lives in Chicago. He is the winner of the Nelson Algren Literary Award, a Pushcart Prize, the Great Lakes Book Award, and a finalist for the Story Prize. He is the author of several novels and short story collections including *Marvel and A Wonder, Office Girl, The Great Perhaps, The Boy Detective Fails,* and *Hairstyles of the Damned.* He is a professor in the Department of Creative Writing at Columbia College-Chicago. "Absolute Beginners first appeared in *Chicago Magazine.*

JOHN McNALLY – is author of eight books, including *Lord of the Ralphs*, a Young Adult novel; *Vivid and Continuous: Essays and Exercises for Writing Fiction*; and *Ghosts of Chicago*, a collection of short stories. His collection of personal essays, *The Boy Who Really, Really Wanted to Have Sex*, will be published in 2017. A native of Chicago's southwest side, John divides his time between North Carolina and Louisiana, where he is Writer-in-Residence at the University of Louisiana at Lafayette.

RJ ELDRIDGE – is a writer, multidisciplinary artist, curator, educator and thinker. A graduate of the University of South Florida's graduate program in Africana Studies, where his studies focused on literature and critical theory, Eldridge has engaged widely on the role of the arts in constructing identity, and seeks to expand the dimensions of contemporary discussion on the intersections between performance, history, race, ontology and myth. His current projects inquire about the politics of millennial identity, contemporary racial literacy, and the power of the image to shape and be shaped by both.

SHERWOOD ANDERSON – (1876 – 1941) An American novelist and short story writer known for self-revealing works, Anderson influenced such authors as William Faulkner, John Steinbek and Ernest Hemingway. He lived in Chicago at various times in the early 1900s and was part of the Chicago Literary Renaissance. *Winesburg, Ohio* (1919) is his most enduring work. Anderson published several short story collections, novels, memoirs, books of essays, and a book of poetry. His story, "Brothers" was written during one of his stays in Chicago and appeared in his short story collection, *The Triumph of the Egg*.

CARL RICHARDS – A street poet, Richards ventures the alleys, sidewalks and streets of Chicago sharing his words with any and all listeners. Richards says he received his education from this and that university. His poem, Birdfeeders, was first published in *The Edison Literary Review*.

CRIS MAZZA – has authored over ten novels, four collections of short stories, and two memoirs. Her most recent work includes: *Something Wrong With Her* (2014), and *Various Men Who Knew Us As Girls* (2011) She is widely anthologized as an example of post-feminist, formalist, or contemporary experimental fiction, and she helped coin the original ironic phrase "chick lit" for the edited anthology, *Chick Lit Postfeminist Fiction* (1995). Mazza directs the Program for Writers at the University of Illinois at Chicago. Among her numerous awards are a PEN/Nelson Algren Award for her novel *How to Leave a Country*. Her story, "They'll Shoot You," first appeared in *Trickle-Down Time Line*, published by Red Hen Press.

ERIC CHARLES MAY – is the author of the novel *Bedrock Faith*, which was named a *Notable African-American Title by Publishers Weekly, and a Top Ten Debut Novel for 2014 by Booklist Magazine.* May is an associate professor in the fiction writing program at Columbia College Chicago, and the 2015 recipient of the Chicago Public Library Foundation's 21st Century Award. A former reporter for *The Washington Post,* his fiction has also appeared in *Fish Stories, Solstice, Hypertext, Flyleaf Journal, F,* and *Criminal Class* magazines. In addition to his Post reporting, his nonfiction has appeared in *Sport Literate, Chicago Tribune,* and the personal essay anthology *Briefly Knocked Unconscious By A Low-Flying Duck.* He has taught at the Stonecoast, Solstice, Northwestern University, and Chicago writers' conferences, and in Chicago he's read personal essays with 2nd Story, and That's All She Wrote, and oral tellings at the Grown Folks' Stories and Here's the Story personal essay programs.

CARL SANDBURG – (1878 – 1967) Regarded as a major figure in American literature, Sandburg, a poet, writer, reporter and editor, won three Pulitzer Prizes: two for his poetry and one for his biography of Abraham Lincoln. His most popular poetry collections include: *Chicago Poems* (1916), *Cornhuskers* (1918), and *Smoke and Steel* (1920). His poem "Chicago" first appeared in 1914 in the Chicago journal, *Poetry,* and later in the collection *Chicago Poems.*

FRANK NORRIS – (1870 – 1902) Born in Chicago, Norris was an American journalist, short story writer and novelist. Considered one of the leading pioneers in American Naturalism, Norris is read and studied for his honest depiction of life at the beginning of 19th Century.

His works include *McTeague, The Octopus: A Story of California* and *The Pit.*

AMY NEWMAN – An American poet, critic and professor, Newman is the author of five collections of poems: *On This Day in Poetry History, Dear Editor –* winner of the Lexi Rudnitsky Editor's Choice Award, *fall, Camera Lyrica* – winner of the Beatrice Hawley Award, and *Order, or Disorder* – winner of the Cleveland State University Poetry Center Prize. Newman has received numerous fellowships in poetry and her poems have appeared in such literary journals as: *Poetry, The Kenyon Review, The Missouri Review, Hotel Amerika, Image, The Rumpus, The Laurel Review, Colorado Review, Berkeley Poetry Review, Denver Quarterly, The Gettysburg Review, Hayden's Ferry Review, Willow Springs, Indiana Review, The Carolina Quarterly,* and in anthologies including *The Iowa Anthology of New American Poetries, The Rose Metal Press Field Guide To Prose Poetry: Contemporary Poets In Discussion and Practice, An Introduction To The Prose Poem, Lit From Inside: 40 Years Of Poetry From Alice James Books,* and *The Hide-and-Seek Muse: Annotations Of Contemporary Poetry.* Newman currently teaches at Northern Illinois University. "Bones and Doubt" was first published in *Unsplendid,* and "The Letting GO first appeared in *Midway Journal.*

MIKE HOULIHAN – is a former features columnist for the *Chicago Sun-Times,* where he penned the "Houli in 'da Hood" column. He has written the "Hooliganism" column in the *Irish American News* since 1996. In 1973, he began his career as an actor in with the American Shakespeare Festival in Stratford Ct., and appeared onstage with regional theatres across the country as well as Off-Broadway, on Broadway, on television and in major motion pictures. His one-man play, *Goin' East on Ashland*, ran for over six years in Chicago, and his play, *Mickey Finn*, had its world premiere production at the Royal George Theatre. Mike contributed humorous essays to public radio in Chicago on WBEZ-FM for several years and also appears onstage in Chicago as a stand-up comic and character actor. Mike is also co-host of the radio program "The Skinny & Houli Show" in Chicago on WCEV 1450 AM. He is the author of two books, *Hooliganism Stories* and *More Hooliganism Stories*. "On the Eario" first appeared in *Irish American News*.

NADINE KENNY JOHNSTONE – recently completed a memoir about the risks and repercussions of In Vitro Fertilization. Her work has been featured in *Chicago* magazine, *The Moth*, *The Drum*, and *Pank*, among other publications. Nadine has worked in all aspects of writing: as a literary magazine editor, reporter, fiction contest judge, story performer, and creative writing coach. Find her writing advice at *Beyond the Margins*, *The Review Review*, and monthly at *Grub Street Daily*. She lives in Chicago with her husband and son, and she teaches at Loyola University Chicago.

QURAYSH ALI LANSANA – is author of eight poetry books, three textbooks, three children's books, editor of eight anthologies, and co-author of a book of pedagogy. A current faculty member of the Creative Writing Program of the School of the Art Institute of Chicago, Lansana is a former faculty member at The Juilliard School. Lansana also served as Director of the Gwendolyn Brooks Center for Black Literature and Creative Writing at Chicago State University from 2002-2011, where he was also Associate Professor of English and Creative Writing until 2014. *Our Difficult Sunlight: A Guide to Poetry, Literacy & Social Justice in Classroom &*

Community (with Georgia A. Popoff, 2011) was a 2012 NAACP Image Award nominee. His most recent books include *The BreakBeat Poets: New American Poetry in the Age of Hip Hop*, with Kevin Coval and Nate Marshall (Haymarket Books, 2015) and *The Walmart Republic*, with Christopher Stewart (Mongrel Empire Press, 2014). Lansana has several forthcoming titles, including: *A Gift from Greensboro* (Penny Candy Books, 2016); *Clara Luper: The Woman Who Rallied the Children*, with Julie Dill (Oklahoma Hall of Fame Press, 2017); *Revise the Psalm: Work Inspired by the Writings of Gwendolyn Brooks*, with Sandra Jackson-Opoku (Curbside Splendor, 2017) and *The Whiskey of Our Discontent: Gwendolyn Brooks as Conscience and Change Agent*, with Georgia A. Popoff (Haymarket Books, 2017). His poems, "dead dead-heat on the southside" and "reverse commute," first appeared in *mystic turf* in 2012.

GARY JOHNSON – Gary has been teaching college-level writing and producing for public radio since 1979. "Marquette Park, 1976" is from a novel in progress.

DENNIS FOLEY – A life-long Southsider, Foley is the author of the memoir *The Drunkard's Son* and the foodie guidebook, *The Streets and San Man's Guide to Chicago Eats*, which won the Midwest Independent Publishers Association Award for humor. His work has appeared in such publications as *Poetry Motel*, *The2ndHand*, *The Chicago Red Streak*, *Gravity* and *centerstagechicago.com*. His novel, *The Blue Circus*, is slated for release next year.

VACHEL LINDSAY – (1879-1931) Another player in Chicago's Literary Renaissance in the early 1900s, Lindsay was an American poet considered a founder of modern singing poetry, as he referred to it, in which verses are meant to be sung or chanted. He authored numerous books including *The Congo and Other Poems* and *The Chinese Nightingale and Other Poems*. His poem, "The Drunkard's in the Street," first appeared in *General William Booth Enters into Heaven and Other Poems*.

THOMAS SANFILIP – Thomas' poetry and fiction have appeared in such publications as *the Shore Poetry Anthology, Thalassa, Ivory Tower, Nit & Wit, Tomorrow, Ginosko Literary Journal, Maudlin House, Feile-Feste, Per Contra,* and *Brilliant Flash Fiction*. Five previous collections of poetry have been published -- *By the Hours and the Ye*ars (Branden Press, 1974), *Myth/A Poem* (Iliad Press, 2002), *The Art of Anguish* (2004), *Last Poems* (2007), *Figures of the Muse* (2012), in addition to a collection of short fiction, *The Killing Sun* (2006). Presently he lives in the Chicago area and has written for a variety of other publications, including *Rattle, The Literary Yard, Independent Publisher, Book Page, Rain Taxi, Letter Ex, Filmfax, Film Quarterly, Film Score Monthly, The Journal of Popular Film and Television,* and the *Walt Whitman Encyclopedia.*

BEAU O'REILLY – is co-curator of the Rhinoceros Theater Festival, a frequent contributor to This American Life, and a professor of playwriting at the School of the Art Institute of Chicago. O'Reilly has produced, curated, and directed work at the Museum of Contemporary Art, Steppenwolf Studio, and Links Hall, and has been named one of Chicago theaters "most influential" a half dozen times. In 2014, he curated and performed a program of four short plays by Samuel Beckett for The Poetry Foundation. In 2015 he curated and performed with Judith Harding six original pieces at The Poetry Foundation. One of fourteen siblings, O'Reilly is the author of over eighty original plays and is also a working actor.

TONY SERRITELLA – A lifelong Chicago resident, Tony grew up in a near-south side Italian neighborhood. He is the author of two memoirs, *Book Joint for Sale: Memoirs of a Bookie* and *Conversations with Fritzie*. In writing his memoirs, Tony realized how much he appreciated his youth, friends and family, and how he wouldn't trade the events in his life with anyone else. "Coming Home" first appeared *in Book Joint for Sale.*

PAT HICKEY – A career educator, Hickey taught at Bishop McNamara High School in Kankakee, Illinois and at La Lumier School, in LaPorte , Indiana. In 1990, he began doing fundraising work which he continues at Leo High School. Hickey has a monthly column (PH Factor) in *Irish American News* and has authored two books. He holds a B.A. and M.A. in English from Loyola University of Chicago. He resides in Chicago's Morgan Park neighborhood.

DOMINIC A. PACYGA – Born in Chicago's Back of the Yards neighborhood, Dominic received his Ph.D. in history from the University of Illinois at Chicago in 1981. While in college he worked as a livestock handler and security guard in the famous Union Stock Yards. He has authored, or co-authored, six books concerning Chicago's history. Pacyga has lectured widely on topics ranging from urban development, residential architecture, labor history, immigration, and racial and ethnic relations, and has appeared in both the local and national media. His latest book is *Slaughterhouse: Chicago's Union Stock Yard and the World It Made.*

BEN REITMAN – (1879-1942) An anarchist, hobo king, physician, and ringleader of Chicago's Bohemian speakeasy— The Dill Pickle Club, Reitmam provided medical services to prostitutes and the destitute in Chicago, and other places he roamed. His essay, "Conscription," was first published in Emma Goldman's anarchist journal, *Mother Earth*, in June, 1917.

MAHJABEEN SYED – is a Chicago-based writer with a degree in creative writing. Her work has been in numerous publications including the *Chicago Tribune*, *Newcity*, *The FEM* and elsewhere. When she is not reading through her stack of books and surrendering to her sweet tooth, she can be found working on her novel and book of essays. "How a Muslim Feels about 9/11" first appeared in the *Chicago Tribune*.

IVAN JENSEN – is a fine artist, novelist and contemporary poet. His artwork was featured in *Art in America, Art News,* and *Interview Magazine* and has sold at auction at Christie's. Ivan was commissioned by Absolut Vodka to make a painting titled "Absolut Jenson" for the brand's national ad campaign. His Absolut paintings are in the collection of the Spiritmusuem, the museum of spirits in Stockholm, Sweden. Jenson has published over 500 poems in a variety of literary media in the US, UK and Europe. The poem "Midwest Juliet" first appeared as a short film by the same name, produced by Drop Drop Studios and directed by Cassidy Bisher.

PATRICK FOLEY – A photographer and graphic designer, Foley's 16 photographs in *We Speak Chicagoese* were taken from assorted city locations. He also designed the front and back covers. His work has been showcased at St. Norbert College, in the movie *Not A Stranger*, and his book cover designs have appeared on various literary titles.

OTHER BOOKS BY SIDE STREET PRESS

The Drunkard's Son, by Dennis Foley, $13.95

Recovering from a stab wound, 15-year old Dennis Foley has far too much time on his hands. He can only stare at the hospital ceiling tiles and study the beige painted walls for so long. Foley is forced to confront his past and examine the path that almost led to his death.

Echoes From a Lost Mind, by Carl Richards, $12.95

Asylums, taverns, back alleys, jail cells and more dot the pages of Richard's debut poetry collection.